SCARBEARER

SCARBEARER

SCOTT GRIFFIN & DOUG GRIFFIN

ISBN 979-8-9995331-0-4

For Mom and Dad
You always said you would have writers in the family.
You should have specified that they would be
good writers.

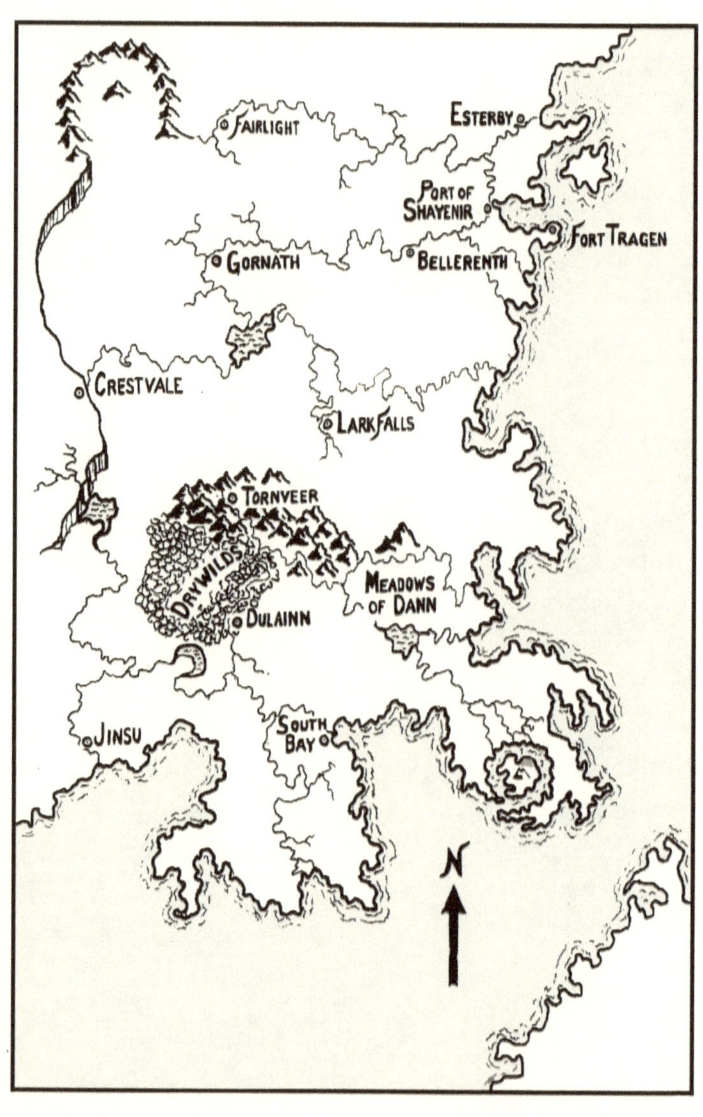

FAIRLIGHT
ESTERBY
PORT OF SHAYENIR
FORT TRAGEN
GORNATH
BELLERENTH
CRESTVALE
LARK FALLS
TORNVEER
DRYWILDS
MEADOWS OF DANN
DULAINN
JINSU
SOUTH BAY
N

CONTENTS

PREFACE

When we committed these words to paper, this world was ours. Events, places, faces and names; we wrote them as they appeared to us. We can describe our world to you as it appeared to us, but what we cannot–and would not–do is to insist on how it appears for you; for in the moment you opened this book a new world was born. A world shaped by your perception and imagination, unique to you and you alone.

So instead of welcoming you only to our world, we welcome you to yours. While the events that transpire in the book you are about to read are common between our worlds, the form your world and the people on it takes is for you; as real and valid as our own. Your world is vast; full of people and stories that only you can tell–and we invite you to create within it.

Enjoy.

Griffin Brothers

PROLOGUE

THE PORTRAIT IN THE RUIN

In the scorched remains of the house, a silhouette flitted in the torchlight. A figure clad in dark leathers paced frantically, as frustrated as he was exhausted. Atenryth had reduced the house and its occupants to cinders but had not returned with the stone; it had now fallen to him to retrieve it. Two stories of rubble and ash—he had sifted through all of it for days. Turning stones, ripping out charred floorboards, digging through the piles of torched books and mementos; scorched and ruined memories of the lives that had been extinguished here.

Nothing.

He had hollowed out the blackened frame of the once-proud house, piles of failure strewn about him. The gem had been here—of this he was certain. Now it was simply gone, ripped from reach once more.

The dark-clad figure grimaced with frustration, kicking furiously at the pile of detritus at his feet.

His toe caught the frame of a portrait, sending it clattering across the floor.

Cupping his face in his palms, he took a moment to collect himself, considering what he could possibly have missed.

He resumed pacing, scouring the ruins when once more his toes met the frame of the portrait. He peered down at it, eyes widening in realization.

Within the seared frame was a lovingly painted portrait, its pigments bubbled and cracked by intense heat. A man and a woman, smiling—their faces were known to him. What he had not expected was the swaddled infant they held between them.

His mind raced. Though the bodies had been removed, he had only seen evidence of two. He wondered to himself if the child could have possibly survived such an inferno; Esterby was not far— perhaps someone had rescued the infant after Atenryth had retreated. The answers were not here, nor was the stone. The child was now the only remaining thread that might lead back to it.

It would have to wait. This stone was lost to him for the moment, but there was still a third to be found. He would return.

Drawing his hood over his head, he strode out into the moonlight.

CHAPTER 1

THE PYRE IN THE DREAM

Cendra struggled desperately for breath through the searing heat. Horrid screams rang through the raging inferno of the house into her room. The flames swelled and roared as the timbers crackled until the screaming faded away, drowned in the fury of the blaze. Panic gripped her as she struggled to rise to her feet, her limbs flailing in futility—she hadn't even the strength to lift her own head. Cendra tried to call out to someone, anyone, but no sound came. Her throat was blistered and hoarse from crying. She kicked her legs violently and saw her feet—those of an infant—swing through the air pathetically. Her heart raced. She could not stand, she could not run, she could not scream—she would die here in this bed, swallowed by flame. With what sad strength she could muster, she flipped onto her side. Through the slightly open door, a flood of orange light cut through the smoke. Cendra strained to see who was beyond the door, but smoke burned her eyes and clouded her sight.

Squinting through the heat and flame, the figure came into focus. Her father, scorched to bone, lay motionless on the floor. At his side, shrieking, tears streaming down her face, her mother reached out to her through the flames. Another swell of flame and cinders and the screams ceased for the final time. Her eyes too dry to cry, her throat too burned to scream, she lay waiting for death under the firelight. As she watched the flames dance, the light gave way to a shadow falling over the door. Filling its blackened frame, an eye—colossal, amber, and unblinking—stared back at her.

Cendra thrashed awake in a cold sweat, panting as she sat upright. She glanced around the room frantically. She was home in her room; not the unfamiliar room from the dream, but the same room she had lived in for as long as she had known —safe once more in her own bed under the blanket she had knitted last spring. She cupped her head in her hands and let out a deep breath. The sight of the smoky gray walls and simple white furniture brought her relief after the horrors of the dream. It was the same dream she had every year on her birthday, but this time it had changed. It had never been so frighteningly vivid, and perhaps most distressing was the *eye*. That terrifying golden eye, glaring into her through the smoldering doorway.

She lingered in bed longer than usual, collecting herself. Pushing the dream out of her mind, she sat at the edge of her bed. There was much to be done, for this was the morning of her *eighteenth* birthday, and as such it was her wedding day—as it was for every young woman in Esterby. It had always been a city of strict tradition. Cendra found a measure of comfort and security in its ways, and yet she could not help but feel somewhat stifled by them.

Like many new adults before her, Cendra found it difficult to resolve her feelings regarding today. She was excited to be an adult, of course. Even the idea of being married to Raleth was somewhat exciting, though she could not say for sure that it was what she wanted. Raleth was kind, funny, and handsome, sure. He was tall and strong, noble and courageous. He had earned some measure of fame recently when he saved a young girl who had wandered off from her mother while shopping in the market on the edge of town. She had been missing for hours, and many had gone looking for her. Raleth found her first; by the time he arrived she had made it all the way to the edge of the woods to the west into the territory of a great black salamander—a massive lizard monstrosity with deadly teeth and claws capable of belching small bursts of fire—that was already stalking her. With no regard for his own wellbeing, he had run in and snatched the child away from the beast, carrying her away and back to the safety of the city walls. He was all of this and perhaps more, but when Cendra thought about him—and especially about *marrying* him—she was not sure how she felt, but it was not what she had imagined love to feel like.

Salamanders had been sighted in the wilds outside of the city for many years. Like most ordinary animals, they were primarily concerned with survival—content to hunt safely within their own territory. However, as with any other magical beast, they could occasionally become pests, straying too close to the city where they found livestock or particularly reckless people as easy prey. Indeed, they were *extremely deadly* pests, as even the slightest bite or scratch from any creature of magical blood was almost assuredly a death sentence. Victims would quickly fall under a gruesome affliction known as the Fever; a brutal sickness that proved fatal in nearly all cases. The rare survivors would suffer perhaps a worse fate—a grim metamorphosis and exile as a reviled Scarbearer. Cendra pondered for a moment if the eye in her dream had been a salamander, but immediately dismissed it. The eye was too large. Rumor had it that they could reach fourteen feet in length, but that eye belonged to something larger. Something truly *gargantuan*.

Repelling a beast of magic was no small feat. Archers in the towers might have been able to drive away those that were young, small, or skittish, but those that were persistent presented a nearly existential problem for a city. City dwellers almost never considered direct confrontation; due to the virulent nature of the magical taint, the risk to guardsmen and soldiers was too great and would assuredly result in catastrophic losses. For these tenacious threats, local leaders would call a Quieting.

A Quieting was a hunt, in a manner of speaking. A town would hire a group of hunters, known as a "Quiet," to vanquish whatever magical beast, or perhaps several, menaced the area. Excitement abounded when a Quieting was called; the town would fill with thousands of people from all over the region. They would come to watch the spectacle of the hunt: a Quiet of Scarbearers battling to the death against a lethal monster. But the festival would last nearly an entire week, with spectators from neighboring communities coming to drink, eat, and spend money. Booths and stalls would line the streets, filled with rare treats and souvenirs.

She had let her mind wander for too long. Cendra rose from her bed and began to prepare for the day. Laying out her gown and other finery, she could not help but wonder if her birth parents were looking down on her now. They had died when she was very young and, though she had almost no memory of them, she thought of them often. As she looked at the gown before her, she hoped they were proud.

She washed up, dressed, and made her way over to her looking glass. Her brow scrunched as she gazed at herself—the small mark adorning her left cheek was puffy and red this morning. She huffed through her nose. *Of course* it would decide to flare up this morning when every eye in the city would be upon her. On occasion it would become slightly irritated and itchy, but it had never been quite this inflamed in the past. The little scar on her left cheek—a small, straight horizontal line just below the eye—had been a feature of her face all of her life. She ran her fingers over it, remembering the fear it used to give her as a child, crying to her adoptive mother Helene that she did not want to become a Scarbearer. Helene would hug her close, reminding her that she had never had the Fever and would hold her tightly until she stopped crying. She did not remember what had caused it; probably some rough play with the other children of the village. Beyond the occasional skin irritation and some self-consciousness, it had never given her any real pain or trouble, and over time it faded into her skin as she came to accept it. She sighed in the mirror and smiled, powdering over the little irritated mark. *Just a beauty mark,* she mused to herself, and finished preparing for the day ahead.

Beyond the door, Helene waited for her daughter, lost in thought. She was beaming with joy and pride, yet could not help but feel some small tinge of sadness and loneliness. This day had been coming for nearly eighteen years. She had raised Cendra as her own ever since the Conclave had formally allowed her adoption. Eighteen years of loving her and caring for her, preparing her for the world—and now that the day was finally upon them, Helene was not sure that she was prepared for it herself.

Her mind drifted back all those fleeting years to the morning when, along one of her long walks she saw billowing smoke in the sky. Fearing that Barrett, Shyla, and their newborn, Cendra, were in danger, she ran to its source—the charred husk of the Faradays' home. She had been far too late to help her dear friends, who burned to death inside their home. But she was not too late to help the wailing infant who lay wrapped tightly in a blanket on the ground some distance from the ruin—by some miracle largely unharmed, save for a minuscule laceration on her left cheek. The Faradays had been explicit in their wish that, should something happen to them, Helene would raise Cendra, even going so far as to have the paperwork drawn up and filed. Yet, the Conclave had been resistant to allowing Helene—herself a young widow, still in grieving—to adopt. They bickered for what felt an eternity about whether Helene would be able to care for a child on her own. She had not taken offense; they had no reason nor way to know that she could provide for the child. Admittedly, there were moments when Helene doubted herself; but from the moment she saw Cendra, sooty, hoarse from smoke, and crying for a mother who could no longer reach her, the babe had taken Helene's heart.

The wound, too, had been a source of much consternation for the Conclave; the nature of the fire and the cut across Cendra's cheek were a mystery. Helene argued to the end of her breath that a lone infant could not have survived a monster, much less the Fever that would follow. After weeks of interviews and piles upon piles of petitions and sworn statements from her friends and relations, the Conclave grudgingly approved. Cendra would have a home.

It had, perhaps predictably, been the source of some controversy in Esterby. Cendra was born to a fairly wealthy couple who had lived outside of the city; near enough to be familiar faces within its walls and yet far enough that it had proven arguable whether they were true citizens who fell under the jurisdiction of the Conclave of Esterby. While there were several voices positing that they were not, the Conclave—perhaps in an effort to manifest its sovereignty over the areas around the city—were quick to make arguments to the contrary. As a consequence of the adoption, Helene would also receive a small percentage of Cendra's estate allotted to her for the child's care; the remainder was to be held by the Conclave until Cendra came of age. While Helene welcomed the funding as it made providing for Cendra much easier, she had not asked for it, nor did she need it. However, this decision had sent yet *another* wave of arguments across the city—arguments that the Conclave had no legal power to seize the estate regardless of jurisdiction, and even fear that the ruling was financially motivated and that Cendra may end up a ward of the Conclave. Ultimately, they approved adoption, though the Conclave members seemed motivated more by the fear of political unrest than by a true sense of justice. In the end, it mattered little to Helene; while she had not cared much for the bickering and posturing, at long last Cendra would come home. That was all that had mattered.

"Mother?" Cendra's voice pulled Helene from her reverie. "How do I look?"

Helene's eyes welled with tears as she looked at her daughter. They had sewn the gown—a radiant pearl white with swirling jade accents—together over the last several months, as was tradition for mother and daughter. Cendra's strawberry blonde hair hung down to her shoulders; Helene sniffled as she swept a stray lock from her adoptive daughter's malachite-green eyes. Around Cendra's neck hung a gleaming golden pendant set with a vibrant faceted scarlet gem, one of the few salvageable heirlooms from her birth parents. Helene had kept it safe until Cendra was old enough to wear it responsibly; Cendra had worn it every day since. Helene struggled not to cry as she looked at the beautiful young woman her daughter had become.

"Just look at you!" Helene's voice was breaking. "You are absolutely gorgeous! I am so, so very proud of you."

Helene took Cendra's face in her hands. Cendra flinched as a searing pain ripped through her cheek. Helene withdrew her hands, concerned.

"Cendra, what's the matter? Are you hurt?"

"It's nothing. My scar is inflamed today, it just seems to be a little worse than usual."

Helene looked at the little mark on Cendra's cheek. She hadn't noticed at first, but she could see now even through the powder that it was puffy and red. Cendra reached up to feel it, but Helene grabbed her hand, stopping her.

"Let's avoid irritating it further, dear. Touching it will only make the pain worse, and by the looks of it, it's likely to bleed if disturbed much further. We don't want that, especially on today of all days." She shook her head, smiled, and placed her hands on Cendra's shoulders. "Don't you pay it any mind. You have it masked pretty well with your powder. I didn't even notice it until you mentioned it. Let's just let it be until after the wedding, then we'll go have it looked at."

They began their trek to the abbey, high on the hill in the center of the city. From their house, they went south to the corner and turned east to cross the street. Cendra tread carefully. A recent rain had left puddles of mud everywhere, and while these shoes were very elegant, they were *extremely* uncomfortable on the rough cobblestone streets. Not a moment too soon for Cendra's aching feet, they made their way onto the proper pavement of the merchants' square.

Cendra had always loved the merchant square. Every day it bustled with activity, friendly faces chatting on the street as they browsed the various shops. The store fronts were all lined up neatly, designed to complement each other with their large paneled windows and inset doorways to showcase their merchandise. Each had its own character; the bakery was decorated with bright pastel colors that were as pleasing to the eye as the smells were to the nose. The alehouse had adopted a more rustic look; the bare wood facade had faded to gray, and the trim work was painted a simple black. This was an aesthetic choice on the part of the proprietor, though, as it was well kept and maintained. A few vendors had carts out on the walk, selling fruits, vegetables, and homemade tools and trinkets. Cendra felt she could spend hours here every day, just taking in the sights and sounds of the city she called home.

"Ah, good morning my dears! Certainly a beautiful day for a wedding, is it not?" Colonel Peldorf removed his high top hat and dipped it in front of him, twisting his mustache and greeting them with a flourished bow as they passed the front of the livery. Curiously, nobody knew where Peldorf had gotten his title, or even whether it was bestowed upon him legitimately or merely a nickname. Cendra had known him as "the Colonel" her whole life. He was a fairly older gentleman, and as far as she could tell people had called him that forever, as if he were born with the title.

The Colonel had hired Cendra a few years ago to help care for the horses in the livery. She loved animals, and horses in particular held a large place in her heart—she often felt they were easier to understand than people. She had very much enjoyed her work there, and would miss it; soon she would be expected to keep house as a married woman.

"It is a fine day, Colonel!" Cendra smiled back before giving him a softly concerned look. "Don't be late now, you will need to be there well before the ceremony."

Peldorf had become like a grandfather to her over her years at the stable, and in his way was the closest thing she had to a father. She thought it only fitting that he be the man to give her away.

"Don't fret my dear, I would not miss it for the world." The Colonel took her hand between his and smiled, then waved and stepped into the livery.

"Oh, there's Orla," Helene said, pointing up the street. "We should stop and thank her on the way."

Orla was standing outside of her linen shop. She had helped them with Cendra's gown, giving them tailoring lessons, advice, and even a wonderful deal on the satin and notions required in its make. She was chatting with a few other women Cendra recognized from the shop, all of them looking at her with wide smiles. Cendra, unaccustomed to this much attention, flushed red.

"I wish they wouldn't stare," she said to Helene while returning Orla's wave.

Cendra felt as if she wanted to hide behind Helene; while she did not consider herself shy, she had never been particularly fond of being fussed over. However, Cendra was aware that today was quite special—not merely for her, but also for all of the people who had helped and supported her. They deserved to enjoy the excitement, so she would try to enjoy it as well.

As they drew close to Orla, Cendra reached out for a hug. Orla squeezed her tight.

"Oh my, Cendra, you look wonderful! Today is the day—we are so very happy for you! Are you ready? Great changes are coming!" Orla spoke so fast, Cendra could not fit in a word. Her excitement was infectious—the rest of the group buzzed around her; questions, praise and well-wishes coming so quickly that Cendra could not process them.

Helene politely intervened, saving Cendra from the onslaught. "I am so sorry dears, but I have to get her to Rumination. I'm sure you understand. We will see you all at the wedding!"

Cendra gave Orla one last hug and waved goodbye to the group. She smiled at Helene gratefully.

Reaching the end of the merchants' square, they arrived at the center of the city. Esterby was founded long ago on a high hill; at its apex stood the massive abbey, its grand limestone walls standing tall against the cerulean sky. The wedding would not be for several hours yet, but for those hours Cendra would be isolated in a sanctuary room in the abbey for Rumination. Tradition held that the bride and groom would separately meditate in this way to contemplate their futures and mentally prepare for their new lives. In the year leading up to this day, there had been many lessons about the Rumination ritual; when to chant, what to chant, and what one must consider during the long periods of silence. Given the frantic pace of the morning, the weight of the wedding itself, the *damnable shoes*, and the distress of the dream still lingering in the back of her mind, Cendra doubted she would be able to focus—but she resolved to try.

Abbot Larkin met them at the doorway. He was a tall, slender man, his blond hair thinning slightly on top, his features sharp, but his face soft and kind. He was relatively new to Esterby, only serving at the abbey for a handful of years. In that time, he had become well known for his friendly demeanor, common touch, and his sometimes controversial subversions of the city's cherished traditions. The twinkle of joy in his eye belied his solemn expression as he welcomed them inside.

"Good morning," he said with a small smile. "What a beautiful day for such a joyous occasion." The abbot handed Cendra a folded garment. "This is your veil. Please don it now and keep it down through Rumination and the wedding ceremony."

Cendra nodded, and did as she was asked. The veil was a mild relief—she would not need to worry about people seeing the blemish on her cheek.

Abbot Larkin led them down a long hallway to an ornate door, its gold-painted trim adorned with winged accents. He took a few moments to prepare Cendra for her Rumination, reminding her of its purpose. " ... and if you feel like you aren't doing it right, it's fine. The Rumination is for you and nobody else. There's nobody hiding in a corner in there judging you," he whispered, with a sly smile and a wink. Then, addressing them both, he said, "I'll leave you now; let you have some privacy. This will be the last time you will be alone together until after the ceremony, and I am sure there are things you want to say." He bowed and departed for the atrium.

Cendra looked at the door before her. "Mother..." she paused. "Did you feel ready? For your wedding, I mean."

"Oh, my precious girl. You have grown into such an amazing young woman, capable and confident. I know you are nervous, I absolutely was; but I have never seen you fail and today will be no different. Rest assured, Cendra; everything will be fine. Go to your Ruminations, and I will see you at the wedding." With that, Helene hugged her daughter and was on her way. Cendra opened the door to the sanctuary and stepped inside.

The room beyond the door was just as the abbot had described: small and dark, lit only by a single candle in the center of the room. It sat on a small alabaster altar where Cendra was to kneel and begin her Rumination. She thought back on the teachings about proper procedure and approached the altar, but as she neared the candle the irritation she had felt from her scar flared wildly; an intense burning like white-hot iron pressed to her cheek. She winced in pain. Her trepidation about the wedding made it difficult enough to clear her thoughts, and it seemed the troublesome little wound was conspiring to make it downright impossible. Cendra drew a deep breath. She could not let Helene down. She steeled herself, stepped to the altar, and knelt.

Pushing the pain out of her mind as best she could, she began her chants. Cendra focused on the dancing flame of the candle, just as Abbot Larkin had instructed. As she watched it flit and sway, she felt a measure of peace; her mind slowly calmed—as did the pain, to her surprise. The further she focused on the candle's soft light, the more her troubles seemed to fade until the flame was all that remained.

Cendra had never considered herself a particularly religious person, despite the Triune being the bedrock of culture in Esterby. The abbey was the nexus of the city and everyone practiced, yet when she found herself there praying or hearing sermons on the Triune, she sometimes felt out of place—as if her participation was merely for acceptance.

Typically, she might have considered the dulling of her pain a trick of the mind, brushing it aside through pure focus, but in this moment she could not help but wonder if there was a touch of the divines in its easing. The relief she felt was deep; it washed over her like the warmth of a hearth. *Is this faith?* she wondered silently to herself. She fell back into her contemplations with a fervor and reverence she had never had before. Cendra became lost in the Rumination.

As the flame continued its ceaseless dance before her, swaying on her breath, her eyes grew heavy. The rhythmic chanting now came without effort, spilling out of her without thought. The room around her faded from her periphery and all she could see was the fire. It swelled, growing larger and larger with each undulation as figures began to take form from it. A small bird, fluttering off the flame into the darkness as a wolf gave chase. Crackling blue sparks appeared in the glow; Raleth's face, then Helene's appeared, growing and changing from one to the other. They were joined by two more faces appearing in the fire; though she only recognized them from her dream, she knew the faces belonged to her parents. They smiled at her through the golden light, and her eyes welled as she looked upon them. The flame swelled once more—*violently.* Cendra shielded her eyes from the intense heat of the fireburst. When she lowered her hands, she saw it. An eye—colossal, amber, and unblinking—stared back at her once more. The searing pain raced across her face. It had returned—no, it *had never left*—and it was time for a reckoning. Thick black smoke clouded her vision as Cendra recoiled in terror and pain, her blood running cold as the grave and hot as hellfire all at once as she stumbled backward and fell, screaming.

With a desperate gasp, she opened her eyes. She was kneeling before the candle on the altar, its little flame still dancing. The room was unchanged, the pain was absent. The burning visions, the agony, all so real, *so very vivid* just a moment ago—gone like a breath on the wind. Myriad panicked thoughts battled in her skull for her attention. Cendra instinctively reached to her face, but caught herself. *No. I can't have it acting up again.* She steadied her breathing, collecting herself. The Rumination was meant to be a time of contemplation to bring clarity, but Cendra had found none. She struggled to process the visions she had seen. Helene, her parents, Raleth, that *godsdamned* eye. *A warning ... ?*

Cendra looked at the flickering candle again; it had seemed to help her focus. *Was it a warning about the wedding?* She had never been entirely sure that this marriage was what she wanted, but she wondered if *anyone* had ever been sure about such a monumental event. The visions raced through her mind; the figures, the faces, the eye—she could not be sure that it all was not merely a dream borne of stress. Even so, her feelings had crystallized.

She dreaded what was to come. *To refuse the wedding?* To the best of her knowledge, in Esterby this would be unprecedented. *Would there be consequences? Would it even be allowed?* Her mind turned to Raleth. It had been clear to her that he loved her, even if she could not honestly say that she felt the same. She desperately wanted not to cause him pain, but for all the confusion of the Rumination, it had made one thing clear—she could not marry Raleth.

She would find him in private before the ceremony, hoping to ease the hurt.

As she opened the sanctuary door, she stopped cold, face to face with the Colonel in full military regalia. Her skin went cold—more time must have passed than it had seemed. She heard the bells in the high tower; indeed, what had felt like a mere several minutes had been the entire Rumination period. There would be no time to find Raleth. She would be forced to abandon him in front of the entire city.

The Colonel smiled, clicked his heels, and with tight military precision, did an about-face. He jutted his elbow, offering it to Cendra. "I told you not to worry, young lady—right on time." he said.

He was obviously very honored to be a part of Cendra's wedding, standing tall and proud. She hoped she was not about to break his heart, as well.

Cendra saw through her veil down the hall as the final stragglers filed through the atrium into the nave—the ceremony was about to begin. Everyone had come in their best: the clerics in their colorful worship robes, friends and family in finely tailored doublets and vibrant gowns, smiles on every face. They had all come to witness her wedding. Her heart beat in her ears as they approached the nave, decorated with large billowing turquoise and cream ribbons and massive bouquets of Sisters' Star flowers. Raleth and Abbot Larkin were already at the altar, but all eyes were upon her. Cendra's stomach sank as Raleth smiled at her euphorically, unaware of what was about to transpire.

Cendra gripped the Colonel's arm tightly and walked with leaden steps down the aisle toward Raleth and Abbot Larkin at the Grand Altar, Larkin already giving his sermon. Her mind raced to come up with a plan when her eyes caught Helene in the front row, a great smile on her tear-streaked face. Cendra wished desperately that her mother could read her mind, that she would have some way to distract the attendees so she could speak privately to Larkin and Raleth, but no—even if she knew Cendra's thoughts, there was nothing Helene could do. No, it would be up to Cendra alone; she had to find a way to stop this without causing commotion and embarrassment. She continued her lethargic but inexorable march. All too soon the moment was upon her—here she stood at the Grand Altar, with naught in her heart but dread. She took Raleth's hand and they knelt together, facing the abbot. Cendra gave Raleth's hand a gentle but firm tug, and then another. He looked over and smiled, unable to see her terrified visage; her veil hid her face from him. There was nothing for it—she would let Larkin finish his sermon and then she and Raleth would talk.

The sermon, while short, carried on for what felt an eternity to Cendra's troubled mind. Abbot Larkin spoke of faith: faith in the Triune, faith in the self, faith in one's partner, and faith in binding love. He spoke of respect: mutual respect, respect of the self, fidelity, honor and trust. Cendra felt herself shrink—in a few short moments, the entire ceremony would be upended. As Larkin's sermon concluded, Cendra found herself wishing it was longer.

"It is time for the recitation of vows. Please turn to each other."

Cendra and Raleth turned to face each other. He had tears in his eyes and a beaming smile on his face. He lifted her veil, and Cendra watched in confusion as his expression distorted. He had always looked at Cendra the way a bride would hope her husband would, softly, with reverence and love. In this moment, his face was twisted in shock and fear.

CHAPTER 2
THE SILENCE IN THE FOREST

It had been four days they trekked through the Drywilds, walking through the days and stopping where they found clearings to rest through the night. For Brandt, the trip itself had been a trifle—in his years of military service, he had grown accustomed to long journeys. His new companion, however, was starting to show signs of wear, and voiced it at every opportunity. Brandt could not discern if this was real fatigue or just the restlessness of youth.

High through the timeless stone branches above, hints of the red of twilight could be seen settling in. The dense parts of the Drywilds were dim at best even at sun's zenith, and soon it would be too dark to travel safely.

"Are we almost there yet?" The voice behind him wielded the droning monotone of teenage boredom like a maul.

"Not far. A few hours more."

They continued through the dense earthen pillars until they found a place where they thinned enough to set camp: two small tents and a meager fire to keep them warm through the night. It was fortunate the trip was nearing its end; they were running low on fuel and nothing in this forest could ever hope to burn. By the light of the fire, Brandt examined the stony foliage around them. Amber light flickered against the white stone trunks, dancing on the face of the ossified leaves. The forests of the Drywilds intrigued him; this journey had been the first time that he had seen them. He ran gloved fingers over the ancient bark and silent, unmoving leaves. What had it been like in ages past? Did these leaves once play in the wind, or had this forest always been dead? Or rather, was it still alive—perhaps thriving in a way he could not perceive? A breeze. There is no rustle, only a quiet howl through the unswaying, petrified growth.

Tannah flopped gracelessly to the ground with a grunt. She sat by the fire and bounced a violet spark back and forth between her palms. "We've been walking for days," she moaned. "There's not even anything to see here. And here I thought you were old and gray."

Brandt briefly shot her a frown before returning to his contemplation of the old woods.

"Nothing? I thought for sure that'd get something out of you."

Sitting down next to the fire with a sigh, Brandt rummaged through his pack for his water flask and took a long draw.

"I heard that around Dulainn the Drywilds aren't dry at all—it's a real green forest. Is that true?"

"I don't know."

"Looking around, it seems impossible. How do you think they could manage to do that?"

"Don't know."

Brandt removed a glove and scratched his face, dragging his claws along his elongated jowls. He had long ago resigned to the futility of shaving away the coarse black and gray fur that had covered him since his Scar manifested. He felt perhaps the itching was the most irritating of the myriad and frightening ways the Scar had changed him; his torso and arms had been grotesquely elongated giving him an inhuman stature, his fingernails had morphed into long black claws, his nose and jaws stretched into a mock snout, and the fur—oh gods, the fur. He had been dreading reaching Dulainn, or in truth any settlement, for there was no mistaking what he was, and most certainly no disguising it. Tannah had no need to worry about blending in; or rather, she wouldn't if she were less impulsive. Brandt preferred to go unnoticed when possible, at sharp contrast with the reckless youth he now found himself saddled with. They had stopped at a small trading post for supplies before entering the Drywilds, their first and last encounter with other people since she came under his watch. It was a small wonder that the traders were even willing to do business with a Scarbearer, and it had ended rather abruptly after an unprompted and unwelcome display of Tannah's talents nearly set one of the traders' carts ablaze. They were less than a day from Dulainn, and Brandt's stomach churned at the thought of a repeat performance.

His wandering thoughts were ground to a halt by a startlingly loud rumble from a different stomach.

"Guess I'm hungry," Tannah chuckled.

Brandt retrieved his pack from his tent and brought it over to her. Rummaging through it, he produced some dried fish and berries and handed them to her.

"Eat, then sleep. We set out early tomorrow. No sparks."

Tannah snorted. "Thanks!"

She ate as Brandt went to his tent and lay down, hanging his head outside to look up through the canopy, gazing into the sky at the few glinting stars visible through the treetops.

"Good night, Scruffy!"

Brandt closed his eyes hard, hoping sleep would find him quickly.

For all its beauty in the embers of twilight, the Drywilds were radiant in the light of dawn. Golden sunshafts fell on the alabaster fronds as Brandt and Tannah marched on their way toward Dulainn. The silence of the stone forest was pierced by a new sound: rushing water—perhaps a river—not far ahead.

"Brandt!"

He spun on his heel, fearing Tannah had fallen or injured herself, but found her crouching next to one of the monolithic trunks. In her hand she gently held a delicate viridescent sprout, a lone green intruder in the chalk-white forest. In the distance, they heard the rustle of fresh growth on the breeze for the first time since entering the woods. More of these sprouts followed, then individual green leaves on the trees. The pale of the branches gave way to brown and eventually complete, healthy plants interspersed with the stony woods. Brandt could smell earth and grass, and the sound of water drew ever closer.

It was nearly midday when they spotted the first buildings peeking through the now-verdant woods. Dulainn was an emerald bastion of life in the bony and still growth, unlike any city Brandt had visited before, not in terms of size—he had visited far larger settlements—but in how it was built. The city was nestled into the woods, woven into the trees. Paths of cut stone planks from the fossilized trees deeper in the forest meandered around woods, linking large gardens and little houses built of planks of wood and stone. Brandt mused to himself that carpentry, lumbering, and masonry must be one-and-the-same professions here. The wilds in this region were decidedly not dry—a stream cut through the middle of the city, dancing through the trees as gracefully as the footpaths. People carried buckets back and forth between the stream and where they toiled, tending to gardens, homes, and the wild vegetation in and around the city.

Again, Brandt was so lost in absorbing the sight that he had failed to notice Tannah charging ahead of him, rushing to greet a very surprised elderly woman watering her garden. Brandt lurched to catch up but stopped himself, remembering his grim visage. If the people of Dulainn knew that he was a Scarbearer or that Tannah was a mage, he figured the best possible outcome would be getting run out of town. He feared another spectacle and wanted to let the woman go about her work in peace, but they were in need of information. He called out to Tannah to come back, but she either could not or would not hear. He hurriedly drew on his gloves and wrapped his scarf tightly around his head. He would have to hope people here weren't very attentive or prone to questions.

Tannah had already begun interrogating the woman when Brandt caught her, driven by a curiosity about the wonders of the city, a curiosity he admittedly shared, but they had come for a single purpose.

Brandt approached, slouching to try to hide his size.

"A thousand pardons, ma'am. I am sorry for my young friend's boldness."

"It's quite alright," the woman chuckled.

She gave them a curious glance, noticing Tannah's bright blue locks and Brandt's curious wrappings. He was sure they had been found out, but surprisingly she merely turned her attention back to her work.

"Long ago I saw Dulainn for the first time myself. I had questions then, too, as I recall, and to see that exuberance about it in a child again is refreshing."

Tannah's questioning had not finished. "How do you do it? Is it magic?"

"Tannah!" Brandt scolded.

The woman belted a single loud laugh. "No harm done, she is young. No, child, there is no sorcery at play here. What you see is generations of toil, nurturing the wilds. The truth is anyone could do what has been done here with enough patience, work, and devotion."

Brandt cast his gaze across the city. Indeed, the people did their work with ceremonial and almost religious care—cultivating, pruning, watering. As he watched, the more deliberate every movement seemed. Trained. Rehearsed. They did not simply care for the forest to sustain them. This was labor born of love.

"Thank you for humoring Tannah's inquisitiveness. May we ask something else?"

"Of course!"

"We're looking for a man who once lived here. A Scarbearer."

Her brow furrowed as her jovial expression gave way to something far more stern.

"You'll find none here. There are no Scarbearers in Dulainn, nor in any city where sense prevails." She remained fixated on her plants, busying her hands dismissively.

Brandt pressed. "Of course, but I've heard that one once did before turning."

"I have nothing to share on the topic. Be on your way."

Brandt briefly struggled to think of a way to coax something more out of her, but quickly thought better of it—he had neither the talent nor patience for tact. He nodded to the woman and turned to leave, gesturing for Tannah to follow.

"Should we ask someone else?" Tannah offered. "We've walked so far."

"Perhaps," Brandt grunted.

As they started to walk away, the old woman paused. She glanced across the garden she tended so dutifully, fidgeting with her shears. "Wait."

The pair turned back to her.

"What business do you have with this Scarbearer?"

Surprised by this sudden opportunity but hoping to avoid having to broach the subject with any more people than necessary, Brandt proceeded cautiously.

"Employment. We are looking for hunters to defend people from beasts."

She scrutinized them now, looking them up and down. "Your wrappings. I presume then, that you are ... ?"

Brandt parted his scarf just far enough to reveal a glimpse of his wolfish countenance.

The woman's eyes drifted back to her plants. "Once he was a gifted herbalist, well respected in Dulainn. Though he is no longer welcome here, I would not see further harm come to him."

"We certainly mean no harm to him. We merely wish to discuss the possibility of work with him."

Silence lingered for a few moments. The woman sighed.

"Raure is usually at his home, a few miles from town. West by southwest out the city, an hour if you are fleet of foot. He comes to the gate on occasion to trade for supplies, so if you follow the trail he takes here, you will not lose your way."

"Thank you for your help, and sorry to have disturbed you." Brandt and Tannah turned to leave.

"One more thing," said the woman. "If you have any further business in town before you depart, I suggest keeping the purpose of your visit to yourself."

Rather than press their luck any further in disturbing the folk of Dulainn, Brandt insisted on departing almost immediately, much to Tannah's dismay. They stopped only to resupply—he had had to send Tannah into the shop alone as he knew he had already overstayed his own welcome in this place.

Out of the south side of the city they had found the trail they had been told of, a narrow trail barely worn into the woods through repeated use. The growth had lost its color gradually as they passed, the trees morphing once more into fossils. Roughly two hours had passed by Brandt's estimate, and they found themselves on a hill overlooking a clearing in the woods where a little house was nestled near a small, clear pond. A handful of trees around the clearing were vibrantly colored, contrasting sharply against the ash white of the surrounding woods. A neatly maintained garden surrounded one side of the house where, from their distant vantage, they saw a man tending to his herbs with the same reverence and focus they had seen of the people in Dulainn.

The pair made their way down the hill slowly; Brandt did not want them to be perceived as a threat, nor did he wish to suddenly disrupt the man's work. They stopped a few yards short of the fence and watched him, waiting for an opportunity to greet him. As Brandt watched, he observed the man's toil was even more painstakingly deliberate than what they had seen, as he frequently inspected individual flowers, leaves, and stems, delicately raising them one by one into the light in hands clad in curiously thick, oversized leather gloves. Brandt puzzled silently about how the man could even do such delicate work with his hands so encumbered.

With a heavy sigh, the man stood and patted the dirt off his thighs. He was somewhat lanky and gaunt, his skin pale. His auburn hair flowed irregularly, shorn close at the sides and back, the rest mostly cropped to the shoulder, aside from a pair of long braids along each side of his scalp, the two of which reached as far as the man's waist. It wasn't until Brandt noticed the pair of gray eyes—not irises, but whole eyes, swirling like mist encased in glass orbs—that he realized the man was aware of their presence.

"Oh, pardon sir. We came here looking for someone, but found ourselves engrossed in your work. I apologize for our intrusion." Brandt explained, all too used to having to justify his wandering thoughts.

The stranger laughed.

"No need to apologize, friend. It's been so long since I've had visitors. I haven't had any in—" He dipped his head. "Ever, now that I think about it. You two are the first. Gairina, where are my manners? I am Raure Irelos, and it is a pleasure to entertain, well... anyone."

Tannah stepped close, awestruck by the clouded orbs that were the man's eyes. She stepped within a couple paces, and waved a hand in front of Raure's face.

Raure stepped back, staying clear of Tannah's hand.

"Yes, little one. I can see you," he chuckled. "Trust me, this is not the first time someone has seen my eyes and thought me blind. I noticed the pair of you on the ridge."

Tannah, despite Brandt's insistence, lost her ability to contain herself any longer. "You're a Scarbearer, aren't you?!"

"Tannah, please. ..." Brandt muttered exasperatedly through his hand, which was pressed firmly against his face.

Raure's smile did not leave, but faded somewhat.

"Ha! Yes, child. I am." He looked wistfully into his palms. "I am indeed."

"I'm not a child! I'm—"

"Your manner far exceeds our own, clearly," Brandt interrupted. "I apologize. I am Brandt—just Brandt—and this is Tannah Pyxner. She is ... Excited. I admit, despite my companion's bluntness I am surprised you are so open about your circumstance."

"Why surprised?" Raure raised an eyebrow inquisitively. "Surely you both already knew; just as I know that you are similarly afflicted. There is no reason for secrecy, I already live in isolation. There is only one thing that would bring someone here seeking me. All that remains is 'why.' But on the subject of manners, we have strayed into topics that carry great weight very hastily. I was about to prepare dinner. Perhaps we three can discuss over a meal?"

"We do not wish to impose—"

"Ha! Nonsense. The forest provides more than enough for myself and guests. Come!" He bounded enthusiastically to his door. Brandt followed, and gestured for Tannah to follow.

"...I'm fourteen," she huffed quietly.

They ate dinner together at a small carved round table in the center of the little circular house, surrounded by shelves with pots and sacks of an assortment of herbs and vegetables, both fresh and preserved. It was a very humble living space, packed tightly by even the few items Raure needed to live. Given that for a week Brandt and Tannah had been living off only what preserved foods they could fit in their pack, any proper meal would have seemed astounding, but it seemed Raure had a true talent for the culinary arts. Their plates had been scraped clean—twice—of the dishes Raure had prepared. He served dishes they had never heard of made with unfamiliar ingredients. Seared lunapaver filets marinated in an ambercane and firebell reduction with spark cap chutney—savory and sweet with a light playful heat at the tongue that turned to a cool chill at the throat, the tiny pieces of spark cap producing a tingling sensation as they went down. Slices of dark murkwheat bread with starchive butter. They had made polite smalltalk between mouthfuls as they ate but, as Raure picked his teeth with a fine bone pick, he seemed ready to address the business that brought them to his home.

"Now that we have exchanged the obligatory pleasantries and enjoyed a friendly meal, we can get to the heart of the matter. What brings you this deep into the Drywilds seeking an exiled Scarbearer?"

Tannah, tired of being talked over and ignored, answered quickly. "We're trying to start a Quiet! There's just the two of us right now, though, and we don't have the experience to join any teams that have openings."

"That is accurate." Brandt added, satisfied with her summary.

"I see. I know you are a Scarbearer," Raure mused looking at Brandt, "but the child is too young. Either she is not, or the Scar has not manifested."

"For one," Tannah scoffed, "I am fourteen. Please stop calling me 'child.' Also, I have my own tricks."

With a smirk, Tannah brought the index finger and thumb of each hand together and produced a brilliant white spark, drawing it out to a crackling ball of purple and azure that reflected in her ocher eyes, casting a blue glow through the small house. She bounced it playfully between her palms and off her elbows before clapping it between her palms to extinguish it. With a flourish, she tucked a stray lock of hair behind her ear before giving a dramatic bow.

"Tannah ..." Brandt scolded. She looked at him with an icy glare. "... Just try not to set anything else on fire on this trip."

"Ah, a mage!" Raure chuckled excitedly. "This is my first time meeting one. I apologize for my disrespect, Tannah. An impressive display! How long have you been practicing?"

"A few months, ever since I first realized I could."

"And how did it come to pass that you would be traveling together?"

She looked upward, piecing together the chain of events in her memory. "Well, a little while after I got my sparks, Ma and Da said I couldn't stay at home anymore. Said it's too dangerous for people like me in the city, and that it's even more dangerous to not understand what I can do than to try to hide it."

"I've met them. They're good people. They didn't want to send her away, but there are no schools for mages. Since our kind are unwelcome more or less anywhere that isn't a slum, sending her with a Scarbearer was the only option available." Brandt paused, then furrowed his brow at Raure. "You've been peculiarly welcoming to a pair marked by magic."

Raure glanced again at the palms of his long heavy gloves, banded and buckled at the palm, wrist, and elbow. "Well, we have that in common, so why not be welcoming? If we were fated to fear each other, I would be back in my garden at this moment with nobody to talk to."

"Point taken." Brandt had noticed Raure glancing at his hands, noting a subtle sadness. "Since we are discussing business, may I inquire about the nature of your Scar?"

"I'd prefer to hear about yours first if you do not mind—if for no other reason than mine is ... difficult to explain."

"Barghest." Brand said succinctly. He unwrapped the scarf from his head, revealing his beastly face.

"I see. How long has it been?"

"Three years, roughly. Military operation. We marched through a pack's territory inadvertently. Mauled nearly all of my detachment before it was over. Only two survived, myself and one other. He was uninjured. I was injured, but survived the Fever."

Mention of the Fever sent both Brandt's and Raure's gazes to the floor. Brandt recalled his own. Three full days of wracking pain, thrashing with cold sweat. Unable to eat or sleep even briefly for the intense stabbing pain through the entirety of his being. Hellish hallucinations of fire and torn flesh. While beast attacks were not altogether uncommon, Scarbearers were still exceptionally rare, as the Fever claimed nearly all. To die quickly to a beast's claw or fang would be a mercy, if not due the exile, then absolutely due the Fever.

" ... Yes, well. Presumably there are upsides to bearing the barghest Scar, as well?"

"Good for hunting, good for fighting."

"Indeed, and if we are to proceed, both will be crucial—"

A little crash interjected as Tannah, wandering around Raure's home, had accidentally knocked over a small potted plant, which lay broken and scattered on the floor. The small, weak sprout lay on its side in a clump of soil.

"I'm sorry," Tannah said meekly, "I was just looking around and ..."

Raure smiled warmly at her. "It's quite alright, little arcling. That one had seemed to be suffering already. I am not sure it would have made it."

He knelt down next to the little sprout, unfastening the buckles on his right-hand glove.

"What of your Scar, Raure? What gave it to you?"

"I ..." Raure struggled under the weight of the memory. He slipped the glove from his arm. Sickly sage-green veins ran under the skin, his fingertips a deep purple as if bruised in perpetuity.

"It was nearly a decade ago, now." He let out a sigh. "Anora—my wife—and I were ripped from our sleep by our Flost—our son—screaming. We ran to his room, but... but it was already too late. In his room was a creature not unlike a bat, massive with pale fur and luminous green eyes, with naught but smoke between the fingers of its wings. Our son lay halfway out of his bed, slumped on the floor, shriveled and gray. We had not even the time to react before it was upon us, catching Anora's neck with a claw before latching onto me. I struggled with the monster on the floor as I felt it draw the very life from my veins for mere moments before Anora—the sun of all my dawns—slew the beast and saved my life. But we had lost our child. Even then, we were robbed of a chance to grieve. We buried him that night and by morning we had already started to fall ill—the Fever had taken hold. I awoke from three days of pain and nightmares only to find that Anora had been taken from me as well." He paused to wipe a welling tear from his eye. "Whether it is true or just a comforting lie, I am told her suffering was not long—that her Fever had relented before she passed."

"Gods ..." Brandt could scarcely find words. "I am sorry, I didn't mean to dredge up such a grim memory." Raure took a moment to collect himself and smiled. "It is quite alright. If we are all to travel together, you would have to know. Besides, Anora would be furious if she were here to catch me sulking. I can hear her now, 'Knuckle through, Raure.' Even now she is right, but still, I do not know what sin I committed to earn this fate. All that I do know is that my 'gift' ..." He reached down toward the little sprout and gently caressed it in his naked palm; the sickly little plant swiftly turned brown and wilted to nothing.

"... brings only death."

The evening had come and gone as the three talked about the prospect of forming a Quiet. As evening wore into night, Raure had asked them to let him sleep on the thought before giving an answer, and invited them to rest in his home for the night. He did not have spare beds for them, but their bedrolls on the floor were still far more comfortable than sleeping on the ground another night. They woke in the morning to find Raure filling a large backpack.

"Ah, good morning friends. I hope my rummaging was not what woke you."

Tannah sprung out of her bedroll. "Does this mean you're coming?"

Raure paused and glanced around his home with a smirk. "Yes, Tannah. I believe I am. I have lived in or near Dulainn my entire life, but now its unique pleasures are no longer mine to enjoy. It is, perhaps, time I broadened my horizons, so to speak."

She ran over and hugged Raure, shocking a surprised chuckle out of him.

"However, it is difficult to prepare for a journey when I do not know what our destination is. Do the pair of you already have an itinerary?"

Brandt had risen and begun dutifully packing his bedroll away. "Our intent is to make for the Port of Shayenir."

Raure let out a little whistle. "Quite the trek, by foot. Might I ask what we expect to find there?"

"Despite all, I still have some old friends there. We will resupply, and ideally find information on where to look next to fill our ranks."

Tannah glanced around the house, and at the garden out the window. "What about your plants and things here?"

"They will fare quite well, I am sure," Raure insisted with a warm smile. "Nature provides everything they will need. My absence will only give them freedom to grow a bit wild. When I return, a little pruning is all that will be needed."

The trio shouldered their packs.

"Well then," Brandt grunted. "Let's be off."

CHAPTER 3

THE PARIAH IN THE VEIL

Murmurs and hushed whispers swept through the congregation. Abbot Larkin, mouth agape, stared at Cendra's face. The scales were a deep, glossy red, like large polished garnets, uniform in shape. They covered the left side of Cendra's face, parting where the little scar had been on her cheek, as if they had emerged from it. As best as he could muster, he adopted a feigned composure, then raised his hands and called for silence from the congregation.

"Ladies and gentlemen, Cendra is not feeling well. I beg your forgiveness; we will need but a moment to give her some air and try to restore her normally vivacious spirits. Please stay right where you are, we will return shortly."

Raleth remained silent, eyes wide.

"What? No, I feel fine but there is something that I need to talk to you both. ..." They were not listening. Cendra could not fathom why they were so suddenly unsettled. She looked for her mother in the crowd. Unbeknownst to her, it was this very motion that gave those in the front pews their first look at the new scarlet adornment on her face. Several astonished gasps were soon followed by a scream from an appalled Phaela Stonlek, who nearly collapsed from the shock.

Motioning urgently to Helene to follow, Larkin hurriedly ushered Cendra and Raleth back into the antechamber. Helene raced to catch up to them, slipping in just as Larkin turned to close the door. Once they were all in he bolted it shut, and turned to face them.

"Would someone please tell me what is going on?" Cendra's voice was loud, but quivering. She thought her scar must have started bleeding—she raised a finger to her cheek. As she ran it along her scar she felt no blood, nor the soft skin that had always been there; she felt only the hardened ridges. "Wh– What!?"

"Well, Cendra, I'm afraid ... Well ... You see, this is not an easy thing to ..." The abbot's voice shook as he struggled trying to find words that might soften the impact of what he had to tell her, and failed.

The tremble in his voice made Cendra's heart race. Her stomach turned—she felt as if she was going to be sick. "What? Please just tell me!"

"Cendra," he began, then halted. "Come to the mirror, there is something you need to see."

He led her to the corner of the room where a full-length mirror stood, used for uneasy brides and grooms to quickly check their appearance before the ceremony.

Horror. The face that stared back at Cendra was hers, and also not. Under her trembling hand, her fingers rested on the crimson scales, hard as stone; an iridescent sheen undulated across them under the torchlight. They had claimed nearly the entire left side of her face, covering her entire left cheek from just below the eye to under the jaw, encroaching on her temple, forehead, and neck. She fell to her knees.

"Scarbearer!" An echo of an old memory flashed across her mind. She was a child playing Untouchable in the street with other children of Esterby. Her "beauty mark" saw her designated the "Scarbearer" more often than not. She would chase the other children, trying to catch them as they ran and screamed in mock fear. Not long after, she would see the reality for the first time when a young man turned one morning. While his name and face escaped her memory, she recalled vividly how his pleas fell on deaf ears as he fled for his life —while a mob of guards and townsfolk spit curses and ran him out of the city.

Tears fell on her knees.

"It can't ..." Panic had made her voice weak. "No. No—I've never been touched by any of those monsters—I've never even seen one! I am not a—"

Helene cut her off, fighting back her own fear.

"Yes, that's right! To be a Sca–" She caught herself on the word. "To *turn*, her blood would have had to have been drawn by a beast of magic." She exhaled sharply. "It's never happened."

Abbot Larkin's expression softened. "Listen, I believe what you both are saying, but something has *clearly* caused these scales to appear that we do not comprehend. We need to understand some things, and *very quickly*—some of the congregation has already seen and they will no doubt sow panic imminently." He turned to Helene, choosing his words cautiously. "Where did Cendra's 'beauty mark' come from?"

Helene paused and looked at Cendra, trying to avert her gaze from the scales.

"I ... In truth, we don't know. It was there when I discovered her, after the fire." She turned to Larkin and saw the concern in his eyes. "That means nothing though! The wound was fresh—no more than a day old, and she never had the Fever after being found."

"If that's true, then she can't be a Scarbearer!" Raleth had finally snapped from his petrified stupor, shouting as if trying to convince himself as much as anyone else.

"She never fell ill in the days after she was found?" The abbot tried to mask his doubt in his inflections.

Helene's stomach knotted. "No more ill than would be expected; she was an infant who had just survived a house fire and was all alone out in the elements."

Abbot Larkin ran his hands down his face. "We cannot concern ourselves with what we do not know. What we do know is that Cendra does indeed have a Scar that has manifested these scales —and indeed, on the day she reached adulthood, just as it would have happened for a Scarbearer." He walked over to Cendra, kneeling beside her and looking her in the eye. "I do believe that you believe what you say is the truth, and I desperately wish this were not happening to you; but whether we believe it or not does not matter at the moment. I fear there are not many outside that door who will."

It was then that they noticed the muted upheaval that was taking place outside in the Great Hall. People had begun clamoring at the door of the sanctuary, arguing loudly. Abbot Larkin stood and looked at Helene, urgency in his eyes.

"We don't have the luxury of time to deliberate on the matter further; we already know what is outside that door. Alderman Stonlek's wife was in the front pew and has already seen Cendra's scales. I heard her shouting the accusation. If I know her husband, he has already ordered the Colonel to ready the militia, and is now working his way around the room planting seeds of fear—fear that if Cendra is not driven out, any of them could be Cendra's first victim and the rest would soon follow. Not to mention your own kin, Raleth; what do you wager your parents are doing right now?"

Raleth could not look him in the eye. He knew the answer but was stunned beyond speech; no doubt they were right at the Alderman's side, stoking panic. The silence accentuated the growing commotion beyond the door.

"I am *not* a Scarbearer." Cendra rose to her feet, her voice growing in a growling crescendo between sobs. The candles around her flickered with each word as she turned to face them, fear and fury flashing in her eyes. "I am *not* a Scarbearer. I AM NOT *A MONSTER!*"

The sconces on the wall flared as her voice reached a roar that rattled their guts.

Larkin's eyes went wide as they lingered on the sconces for a moment. He drew a long breath and slowly let it out, attempting to expel his anxiety. He placed a hand gently on Cendra's shoulder. In his time in the city, he had been counsel to many, and Cendra's temper was not new to him. Fortunately for the people of Esterby—and now especially for those in this room—he had always possessed a talent for mollifying people, easing their fears and worries. It was a trait that had served him well as abbot. Though Cendra did not know, she had also taught him something of value over his years as abbot—the importance of sincerity. He knew from experience that Cendra would disregard everything he told her if she sensed even a touch of pretense. Smiling, he looked her in the eye and spoke.

"I know that, Cendra. I know you. I am only telling you what those people are thinking. They are frightened, and fear unchecked is dangerous. You need to know what you will be facing if we walk out that door."

The hostility in the nave grew loud and furious. Fists pounded on the sanctuary door as it elevated to a fever pitch.

"Send her out, Larkin!" Stonlek's voice was thick with theatrical forcefulness.

Larkin knew Stonlek well—he would not want the door to open, the coward that he was, but a good politician knows when to play their role at the front of a mob. Larkin felt a sense of disgust. He had always believed that courage was found not in clenching a sword, but in open arms.

"We can't stay in here much longer. They aren't just going to leave.There's nothing else for it." He walked to an old cabinet behind his desk. "There is no choice but to flee. There are tunnels that run beneath the abbey, winding through the cliffs out to the coast. A little secret shared with me by Abbot Anselm before he passed the title to me." He pulled an old map from the cabinet and spread it open across his desk. "Their purpose has been lost to time, but they've been handy for the occasional undisturbed stroll along the shore. I am so very sorry my dear—there is but one answer, and that is to flee. We will use the tunnels to conceal your flight from the city; at least this way you will be safe." The door began to splinter as fear filled the room. "Grab a candle."

The tunnels were very old—hundreds of years at least by their estimate, but meticulously carved. Whoever had cut them took great pains chiseling them from the limestone. The walls and ceiling were cut almost completely flush and smooth, braced with iron and meeting at perfect right angles. Craftsmen of long ago had placed torches at regular intervals, mounted in arched recesses cut into the walls specifically for them at regular intervals along the entire length of the tunnel. The curious wedding party lit the first few they found and used them to light their way as they hurried down the corridor. The torches provided great comfort as the mice and other small creatures scurried away from the light as the group moved along. The torches were also helpful for burning cobwebs out of their path, as the tunnel was full of them.

Larkin brushed a particularly thick cobweb from his face. "I suppose it has been some time since I last passed this way."

They hurried through the tunnel, which ran east for several hundred meters, emptying into a large natural cavern. There they stopped momentarily, trying to adjust their eyes to the darkness. The vast cave seemed to thoroughly swallow the torchlight, the walls and ceiling beyond its reach. Only the rugged ground of the cave directly in front of them was visible, a stark contrast to the precisely hewn floor of the tunnel. Their path along the craggy floor was riddled with obstacles; just within the area that their torches lit, they could see large boulders that must have fallen from the unseen ceiling, great stalagmites, and sheer drops along the perilous path.

"Well, I never said it was an *easy* trek, but it is a touch worse down here than I remember," the abbot whispered.

A voice echoed in the distance behind them. "Here! They came through here! I can see their lights ahead!"

Abbot Larkin quickly moved forward to lead the way. "Do not fret. If we hurry now and get enough distance between us, we will be fine."

Shadows from the boulders and dripstones danced along the floor, growing and shrinking with the movement of their torches. Ahead, they could hear water trickling into pools. Behind them, the sound of their pursuers noisily traversing the tunnel.

There was no time to waste as they moved through the dank caves. They moved onward as quickly as they could, slowing down only when the way was made dangerous by the rough terrain or when Larkin had to pause to get his bearings in the natural labyrinth. They would need to put as much distance as they could between them and the following townspeople. It was fortunate that Larkin had a map of the cave; their pursuers could only chase the sounds and lights in the distance.

Larkin finally spoke, breaking what felt like an eternal silence. "This all looks familiar. The mouth of the cave should be just ahead."

The noise of their hunters had faded to nothing in the depths of the cave. Cendra thought for a brief moment that perhaps the townspeople had recognized the futility of navigating the cave system and had given up on the chase, but she knew deep within that they would not be so easily dissuaded.

As the mouth of the cave came into view, Cendra could see the light was waning as the embers of twilight settled into the sky. They exited the caves as the sun began to sink on the horizon. There, they sat to rest and consider what would come next.

"I have a friend in the Port of Shayenir, " Helene said with trepidation after a long period of quiet reflection by the group. "Her name is Fionna. She lives in Stone Row, the slums that run from the south side of the city to the end of the harbor. It is not a gentle place, but I know that Scarbearers are typically left to their own devices there—even if only because the people there are too downtrodden to care."

"And how would you know this?" Larkin asked, his eyes narrow.

"My friend ... Fionna. She is a Scarbearer. I know that she would take us in and help Cendra through this." Helene glanced at Larkin, expecting some sort of admonishment or at least some comment about having connections with Scarbearers. His warmth and gentleness aside, he was still the abbot, and Scarbearers were abominations.

"Yes, it's your only option, but," Larkin gave Helene a heavy look, "Cendra will have to go alone. You need to stay. You have to be here to represent her before the Conclave. If there is any hope of bringing Cendra back, or at least getting her inheritance to her, it is through you."

"Damn the inheritance!" Cendra and Helene exclaimed in unison.

"Do you know how hard it is to survive as a Scarbearer out there?" Larkin looked at Cendra, who was about to explode, and showed her the palms of his hands. "Whether or not you are in fact a Scarbearer will make no difference. The people out there will see a Scarbearer. It will be a struggle all the way. You will need that money."

Cendra could see in Helene's face that she knew he was right. A lump of panic grew in her chest as she watched her mom's eyes well up. She knew what Helene was about to say, and did not let her.

"I just want to go home!" Cendra cried. "These people are our friends and neighbors, they know me, they know I'm not a Scarbearer, nor am I a danger to them. We can just go home and wait for everyone to calm down."

She wanted so badly to forget all this; to fall into her bed and to wake up tomorrow in her safe, familiar room, seeing all the familiar smiling faces in the marketplace. What she wanted mattered little. In the depths of her heart she knew the truth—there was no returning. Scarbearer or no, that is what the people of Esterby would see, a monster to be hunted down or driven away.

"They have likely already searched your home," Larkin asserted. "In all probability, they have torn it apart looking for you. Once fear takes hold, it overruns common sense. I regret deeply that it has come to this, but you have to go for your own safety. Find Fionna, and find out what is happening to you. For all we know, it could come to pass that you are right; that this is not a manifestation of a Scar, but you need to find that out and be able to convince people here of that if you want to come home safely."

"But I can't just leave!" Her voice gave way to choking sobs as the tears fell. "My life is here. Everything I know and love is in Esterby! Even if I wanted to, I have nothing! No clothes, no food, no money ..."

Helene reached into her bag and produced a pouch.

"I was going to give you this after the ceremony. I've been saving whatever money I could from the Conclave's allowances. I figured it's really your money; it was never mine and it wasn't theirs to give to me to begin with." She handed the pouch to Cendra. "I knew it was nothing compared to the inheritance you would have received from the Conclave. I really thought it was silly to do it at times, but now ... Now I think it will prove valuable, after all this. You need to take this and use it to find your way—get to Fionna. Find a way to make a living. I'll stay here and work on your behalf to convince the town and the Conclave that you are not a threat. I swear ... I will find some way to bring you home."

The weight of her situation had sunk into Cendra's chest. She wept openly, burying her face in her hands. "Why ... Why is this happening?"

"Oh, my darling Cendra." Helene took her daughter's hand. "If I could, I would bear all of this for you. If there were any way I could spare you this, I would in a heartbeat—but I can not. I cannot even imagine the fear you must have, but I know in my heart of hearts that you will be fine. I have never seen you fail. You can do *anything*, and you *can* do this. You will come out of this stronger than ever—but it is something you must do for yourself."

Though still she wavered, even at her lowest moment her mother's words bolstered her resolve. Cendra lifted her shoulders. They were right; there was no other option. She had to leave, and if she had to leave, she would at least try to ease Helene's pain as much as she could. She straightened her back, determined to be strong and make her mother proud. She looked over to Raleth, who had scarcely uttered a word, his face pale and distant.

"Cendra, I'm sorry. ... I can't. ..."

"It's alright." She smiled as warmly as she could muster. "I was hoping to find a way to tell you at the service that I couldn't go through with the wedding. It was made clear during my Rumination. It was not meant to be."

Raleth wiped a single tear from his eye and chuckled sheepishly, trying to mask his hurt. "I believe that is now clear to all of us. Don't worry about me—you have more than enough to deal with right now. I am so deeply sorry for this. I do care for you, I will help your cause here any way I can."

"Please watch after my mother—she will need help."

"I will; I swear it."

"As will I," Abbot Larkin added. "Cendra, you must be off now; it won't be long before someone finds their way down here. Travel south—stick to the shore line. It will lead you to the Port of Shayenir in a few days. Bakka nuts, fieldberries, and pepperleaf are all in season, you should find plenty on your path. If you encounter anyone along the way, keep your veil down and give them a wide berth."

"Find Fionna as soon as you arrive," Helene urged. " Go to the fountain in Torvii Square. I will send word ahead for her to meet you there. Repeat it to me."

"Torvii Square. The fountain." Cendra choked the words out.

"Good!" Helene sniffled as she embraced Cendra for what she hoped beyond hope would not be the last time. "Please ... please be careful, Cendra."

Faint voices emanated from inside the cave.

"They're upon us. Go. Now!" Larkin whispered.

Cendra's body lurched, frozen in hesitation as the weight of reality took hold. This was to be the day that she began her own life, safe at home in the walls of Esterby with her family and friends. Instead she had found herself an exile fleeing her home, an armed mob at her heels. With no small amount of effort, she willed herself finally to move. She ran south into the woods so the trees might cover her flight.

Within moments, a handful of shouting, armed men exited the cave. They rushed forward brandishing whatever weapons they could find, from spears to clubs fashioned from broken table legs. They stopped abruptly when they saw the group standing near the mouth, their bravado faltering momentarily before noting Cendra's absence.

"Raleth! Are you harmed, boy?" Raleth's father, Gareth Prentish, had been the first out of the cave, marching directly toward them.

"No, Father, I'm fine, she ..." Raleth glanced over his father's shoulder and saw Larkin shake his head subtly. "She's gone. She was gone as soon as we got out of the cave."

"Where has she gone?"

"She sprouted wings and flew away," Larkin answered.

The group of men gasped, raising their eyes and weapons to the sky. Gareth's eyes widened then quickly narrowed.

"I suppose you think yourself clever, Abbot, but I am not in a gaming mood. That witch had my boy! She could have ..."

Larkin cut him off. "What is it that you would have us say? She made her way out of the cave before us, and she was gone by the time we made it out. None of us were particularly eager to give pursuit ourselves."

Gareth eyed him intently while he considered his story. He then turned to a visibly distraught Helene. "And you—you are her mother. Where would she have gone?"

"I ... I do not know, she has never left Esterby!" She broke down crying. "She will have nowhere to go."

The tears and sobbing were genuine, which made the lies easier to deliver. Larkin could not help but smile slightly at Helene's performance, but he hid it quickly. The rabble searched for a short time, but did not venture far. None among them truly had the courage to confront a Scarbearer, masking cowardice with feigned boldness. Tonight they could go into the tavern and tell their heroic stories of saving their city from a rogue Scarbearer, milking free drinks and stroked egos from the other townsfolk.

Cendra trudged several miles in the dark of dusk, keeping within the wood but always maintaining sight of the shoreline. Her breath was ragged, fatigue exacerbating the fear and anxiety that gripped her heart. Branches whipped and cut her in the darkness, her feet fumbled over stumps and felled trees. She wept as she dragged herself through the undergrowth, sobbing for all that was now lost to her—her family, her home, her *life*. Her pace grew brisk and her sorrow smoldered with every step before finally giving way to something else—*anger*. An anger that was stoked with each scratching thorn, every ankle-turning branch, every biting insect. Her foot caught the ragged stump of a long rotted-away tree and she tumbled headlong into the darkness, sprawling in the brush. She dug her fingers into the mud, slowly clenching her fists as she pressed herself off the ground to her knees, bawling and burning in pain and fury.

The forest warped and shimmered in her vision as her breath came in rushed huffs. She crushed her eyelids together—*and screamed*. She screamed with the whole of her body, her rage pouring forth from every pore. Intense heat enveloped her as the wrath within her burst forth, given form in roaring flame. She screamed until naught was left in her, her energy fully spent. Exhaustion took hold—she heard the roar of flames and the crackle of the trees as her eyes rolled back. All was dark.

CHAPTER 4

Two Lights in the Darkness

Tannah was glad for the new company on the long walk to the Port of Shayenir. In the time she had known Brandt, he had proven to be more stoic, dour, and silent than any person she had ever met before. In fact, Raure may have spoken more in the three days since departing Dulainn than Brandt had since they had met, sharing jokes and stories of his life in the Drywilds. He often asked Tannah questions about being a mage, most of which she was not yet able to answer. She realized she had never really considered just how much of what she now was that she did not understand.

For his part, Brandt was thankful that there was now someone else around for Tannah to talk to. The distraction afforded him focus, freedom to concentrate on building at least a rough plan for what would come next upon reaching their destination. They would need to take stock of what they had, and for outfitting a Quiet they would need to purchase supplies and equipment. Registration fees. Food. Shelter. For all of this though, fundamentally they needed work—what money they had would not suffice. Work would be hard to find, however, as they were still at least one person short of a functional Quiet. Attempting any real contract with a headcount of three would likely see one or all of them dead.

Tannah was again bouncing a little purple spark between her palms as she walked—her favored way to occupy her mind.

"What have you learned to do with your lightning so far, Tannah?" asked Raure. She paused, letting the spark fizzle out in the air. She was not sure how to answer.

"Mostly just little tricks like this; they're fun. I haven't really thought about what else I can do."

He looked at her with a smile. "There must be a plethora of applications for a talent like that. With a little creativity and experience I wager the potential is positively limitless, little arcling."

"She will need to learn quickly," Brandt muttered. "A challenge, given our lack of understanding."

He looked to the horizon. They would soon be approaching Torenvir, nestled in the mountains, where they would stop briefly for food and rest. Perhaps it was time for some training. Time to learn something practical.

Cendra gasped herself awake on the cold ground of the forest. Even before she opened her eyes, she was overwhelmed by the smell of damp ash. She struggled to a seated position and surveyed the woods around her. Everything nearby had burned; the trees stood charred and blackened and the forest floor was smothered in ash, turned to a dark gray mud by the morning dew. Panic gripped her as she remembered her last moments of consciousness. She frantically inspected her body, patting herself down and looking over her skin. Nothing. Aside from the scratches and bruises she had earned running through the forest, she was wholly intact. Even the gown she wore, though tattered by the brush of the forest, had been spared from the fire. Her heart pounded in her chest as she surveyed the charred landscape, thumping loudly in her skull. The burst of flame had engulfed a circle roughly ten feet across, centered on her person; anything beyond that had been spared, as had the ground directly under her.

Cendra tried in vain to grasp what had happened. No sense would be made of it. She knew she had felt the heat, an intense heat that seemed to emanate from her very core, but she had felt no pain and no burn as it had erupted from her body. Her body grew warm and her hands began to sweat. Her breath came in rapid gasps as fear sank into her mind. Perhaps it would happen again—

perhaps it was happening now. Perhaps this time she would not be spared by the fire. She could not catch her runaway breath; she sucked in air in harsh gasps but felt there was no air to breathe. She cupped her face in her hands, hyperventilating into her palms.

Monster. The breathing gave way to sobbing as the word thrummed through her mind. *MONSTER.* She released a muffled scream into her clenched fists—no fire came.

No. She thought of the candle and tried to empty her mind. Her chest relaxed as her breathing normalized. She did not have the luxury of time to indulge in self-pity; she was alone and on the run with no food and no water, and hunger was setting in. She had naught but the clothes on her back and the coin pouch Helene had given to her. She knew now that there was no other choice, she must find her mother's friend, Fionna. That was her only chance now. If she could hide her face, perhaps she might be able to buy food and supplies somewhere along the way. Wasting no time, she packed up her few belongings and set off for the Port of Shayenir.

Shink. Brandt plunged the tip of his arming sword into the clay several paces from the fire, standing it upright.

"There," he pointed. "See if you can hit that."

No sooner had the words left his mouth than an azure spark hit the ground immediately between him and the sword, leaving a small scorch in the dirt. He shot her a glare.

"TANNAH—" He seethed before catching himself. "*Please* wait until I have cleared the area."

Tannah's head sank at the scolding as Raure attempted and failed to stifle a snort, earning him a seething glare as well. With a grumble, Brandt walked a few yards from where he planted the sword.

"Now. Focus. Try to hit the sword."

A deep breath. Tannah squared herself, focusing her eyes on the hilt of the sword. After calculating in her mind for a few seconds, she loosed a crackling cerulean orb in its direction. It flew straight and true and, just as it appeared it would find its mark, veered sharply to the right toward Brandt who had only an instant to dive clear before it left another small scorched crater where he had stood.

"I'm sorry! I'm so sorry! I don't know what ... I don't—" Tannah was already on the verge of tears.

Brandt was on his feet with fury in his eyes, his fur bristling in the moonlight before he caught himself. He ran his hands down his face as he regained his composure.

"It's alright. It's fine. You are still a child and you don't know how this works." He let out an exasperated sigh. "Hell, I don't know how this works. I shouldn't even be attempting to teach you, but there are no options and you must learn."

They sat in weighted silence for a moment that felt like an eternity.

"An observation, if I may," Raure chimed.

Brandt slumped to the ground next to the fire. "Go on."

"I know nothing of magic. Certainly no more than either of you. However, I do know life, emotion, and the connection between. I watched, and your eyes never left the sword—yet I do not believe you were thinking about the sword, little arcling. You were thinking about our surly friend, weren't you?"

A deafening pause.

"Well, I suppose. ... I mean—I was afraid I might hurt him." She fidgeted anxiously.

"It's alright, young one. What I posit is that perhaps your magic is called to the object of your thoughts. Perhaps it is not enough to focus your sight; you must also focus your mind."

"I—I can try," she stammered with wet eyes as she made to stand again.

Brandt furrowed his brow and scratched the fur on his chin. "No, I believe that is enough for tonight. We rest. Tomorrow we continue on and we will try again when night falls." He stood, picked up his pack and walked to his tent. "And Tannah, I ... I am sorry."

The sun had not yet breached the horizon when rustling leaves outside stirred Tannah from sleep. She wasted no time getting ready; if Brandt was up already, she did not want to keep him waiting. Though it had not been her fault, she felt in her heart that she had disappointed him, that she had failed. She resolved herself to work diligently so that it would not happen again.

Pulling the tent flap back, she peered through the opening to find not Brandt, but a small creature, a bulbous, waddling ball of fur. It stood about a foot and a half high on tiny cloven hooves, its four short legs barely visible under long tawny fur that hung nearly to the ground. It cooed and chirped cheerfully as it wandered the camp, sniffing the ground intently. Tannah sat silently, smiling as she watched from her tent.

The little creature's sniffing intensified as it reached the base of a tree—the tree bearing the branch Brandt had selected to hang the bags containing their rations. Its coos grew louder as its little forelegs tapped at the trunk of the tree, the little snout peering out from behind the fur flaring intently. The noise roused Brandt and Raure, who exited their tents and watched on in amusement. As Tannah made her way over to them, another of the little animals crossed between them, heading for the first.

The group chuckled quietly as the two little beasts hopped futilely up and down, trying in vain to reach the food stores in their packs. It was only when five more of the fluffy little beasts appeared that the smile began to fade from Brandt's face. He watched as they hopped on top of each other, making a wobbling tower that came well short of the packs. He laughed at their folly, but fell silent when the top furball jumped to the top of the packs and climbed into his. When it emerged with his hardtack and jerky and fell to the ground, Brandt gave chase.

Raure and Tannah watched as they bolted around the camp. While Brandt was faster, the furry thief could turn with much more agility; it deftly avoided Brandt's lunges as it squealed, the jerky flopping wildly in its snout.

"Some help, please!" Brandt pleaded, "Unless you'd like to share your food."

They could not help but chuckle at the absurdity as they joined in the chase, but the laughter was short-lived. They proved no more successful than Brandt; as the chase stretched on, the laughs gave way to grunts, curses, heavy breathing, and finally exhaustion as the fuzzy miscreant slipped fingers, ducked between legs and darted between tents. In the end, their fluffy burglar waddled briskly away as the group doubled over, heaving for breath—realizing too late that they had strayed from camp in their pursuit. Frantically looking back to their camp, they watched in dismay as the last two of the creatures scurried away, their food packs empty on the ground.

"No!" Tannah jogged ahead and searched the mess that had once been the contents of their packs. "They took everything ..."

Raure let out a little whistle as he laid a palm on Tannah's shoulder. "Resourceful little devils, it seems. All will be well, though; the land has a way of providing. We will get by. Trust in nature." His voice was full of reassurance. "Brandt, how far to our destination?"

Brandt shook his head. "Three days, maybe four. Too far on empty stomachs. Nature will have to provide fairly damn quick."

The day had gone slowly by as Cendra trudged on toward her destination. She cursed aloud at her unbearable situation and those who had banished her into it, when a sound from behind the trees and brush to her left caught her attention. She paused to listen. Hearing nothing after a few moments she carried on, slowly and quietly with her attention focused toward the area of the sound. Then it returned—a grunt, followed by the rustling of leaves in a wild tackberry bush.

"*... Hello?*"

The rustling of the tackberry leaves ceased for a moment—an obvious reaction to her voice, but soon continued as if unaffected by it. Cendra waited, frozen in place, scared to move. Whatever was behind the bush was small enough to be hidden completely by it, but large enough to shake it violently—she wagered at least her size or greater.

With another grunt, the leaves went quiet again, though only temporarily. Mere moments later, with a resurgence of rustling leaves, a bear cub emerged. A smile crossed Cendra's face as she watched the little cub wage a playful attack on a butterfly. Pouncing at its target, front paws stretched out wide above its head, the cub came down short, lying on its belly as it watched the butterfly peacefully flutter away. Forgetting the fleeing quarry, it rolled to its back and worked its shoulders and hips back and forth in unison, scratching its back on the ground.

A little smile played on her lips as she continued to watch as the furry creature played and somersaulted around the clearing. Looking closer, she noted its unusual appearance; its fur emanating a soft blue glow, flowing back and forth as if on a wind that was not there. The realization flashed across her mind; her amusement falling to abject terror.

Where is the mother ... ?

A snarling roar from behind; an unnatural bellow that sent shockwaves rippling through the air. Dust and leaves flew through the air at a stinging velocity as Cendra turned. The thunderhide towered behind her, standing tall on her hind legs at thrice Cendra's height, staring her down at the distance of a stone's throw. It released another gut-wrenching blast; the force rolling Cendra backward. She rolled to all fours, crawling frantically away from the gargantuan mother bear.

Stumbling to her feet, she burst into a sprint. Cendra could hear the thunderhide's snorts and the colossal thumping falls of its heavy paw pads gaining on her as she raced through the trees. She ran as quickly as her legs could carry her, but lost ground with each step. There was no hope in outrunning the furious mother bear. She frantically scoured the forest with her eyes, searching for any advantage she could find in evading the beast when she spotted a pair of trees, their trunks growing close in a narrow angle. She dove through the narrow gap between their twinned trunks, leaving the bear no time to correct course. The bear's hulking form slammed into their trunks, the trees bending violently, dropping leaves and fruit, groaning, and cracking. They buckled, but they did not break.

The desperate maneuver had bought Cendra precious few moments. She chose the first large tree she could find, climbing as high as she safely could. Clinging desperately to the trunk she watched in horror as the mother bear began to climb up after her, the wood of the tree groaning under its mighty weight. Dread drove Cendra higher up the trunk. The mass of the great beast rocked and swayed the tree; the higher Cendra climbed, the more violent the undulation became. Her grip began to falter.

Cendra halted her ascent and clutched the trunk of the tree with all the might in her. The great bear continued, step by agonizingly slow step. The tree gave a resounding groan and the bear halted. Its gaze wandered from Cendra to the ground; the thunderhide seemed to know that if it climbed any higher the tree would finally give way underneath. The mother bear looked up at Cendra and snarled—then began to descend.

"Ohhh thank the goddesses," she whispered to herself, watching as the beast dismounted the tree. "Go on! Get out of here!"

The cub rejoined its mother at the base of the tree. The thunderhide nuzzled its child and raised beady eyes back up to Cendra and snarled, then led the cub away, deep into the woods.

Cendra watched as they disappeared in the distance. Panic had begun to subside, but anxiety prevented her from descending the tree for nearly an hour after the thunderhide and her cub had disappeared into the wood. Even then, it was only exhaustion eclipsing her fear that finally drove her to make the descent. She slowly climbed down, exiting the tree and collapsing at its base.

After waking at dawn, Cendra had set out quickly, not wanting to be in the forest any longer than she had to be. Now, the beams of sunlight breaking through the forest canopy hung in perfectly vertical shafts, signaling midday and time to stop for lunch. Cendra found a small clearing with a fallen trunk that would serve as a decent place to sit. Her hunger gnawed at her stomach, but she had grown tired of eating nothing but the bakka nuts she had been collecting on the way. She opened the improvised sack she had crudely fashioned from a small strip of cloth torn from her gown and produced a bakka nut she had roasted yesterday, eyeing it ruefully. Larkin had been right, the nuts were ripe and fairly filling. They were roughly three inches long and had a hard, tripartite shell. They had a taste reminiscent of pistachio, but the bakka had a peppery quality that she had found quite nice; that is, until she had been eating them for three days. She pulled the flesh of the nut from its shell, then set the empty shell under a dripping rock. The steady drips pooled in the shell as she—with no small amount of effort—choked down her food. She sat for a long while, resting and enjoying the warmth of the sun while sipping the clear water from the lined up shells.

Her thoughts drifted to the first night in the woods, to the burst of fire. Something buried within the experience dwelled in her memory, something too obscure for her to articulate. A sense of release, perhaps, a purgation or catharsis—or perhaps it had been *control*. A feeling that the flames that were borne of her might somehow be hers to command if she only knew how. It stood to reason; as she understood it, Scarbearers were able to learn to exert control over the abilities that manifested with their Scars. While a controversial subject at best, she had read about Scarbearers often, usually on news posts in the square in regard to local Quietings. "A *necessary evil*," they had been called; they were uniquely suited to save villages, towns, even cities from the threat of beasts borne of magic with the "gifts" inherent to their curse. The people largely feared them just as they feared the wild beasts that menaced them, and thus chose to shun them completely, as her friends and neighbors had done to her.

She shut out the thought swiftly—now was not the time to dwell on it. Her focus was exerting control over the fire—if for no reason beyond preventing an accident that might result in the injury or death of herself or others.

Cendra looked around the clearing and found another fallen tree; dead and dry, it would take to flame easily. She raised her arm before her, her open palm pointed at the desiccated log. She closed her eyes and envisioned the flame erupting forth from her palm—to no avail. Cendra looked into her palm, furrowing her brow. She brought her arm back before violently thrusting her palm toward the tree. Once more, the fire did not answer. She closed her eyes forcefully and concentrated on her target. She saw it clearly in her mind. She brought both hands to her chest, palms out and fingers curled, then thrust them both directly out toward the tree. She willed the fire to come forth, contorting her face with strain. The rustle of the leaves on the breeze was the only response. Her shoulders drooped. Her arms fell to her side. She blushed with the realization of how absurd she must have looked, flailing impotently at a dead tree. She glanced quickly around the wood to confirm there were no witnesses to her ridiculous pantomime.

"Idiot!" Quickly gathering her bearings as well as her meager belongings, she turned south and set off again for the Port of Shayenir. By her estimate, there remained only a little over a day on her trek. There, she could finally get clothes, provisions, and some decent food. She stepped out of the clearing and back into the woods. Behind her, a wisp of smoke drifted skyward from the jagged end of the fallen tree.

The last glimmers of sunlight were fading on the twentieth day of their journey; from the clifftop where they made camp for the last night they watched its final embers dance on the distant waves of the Oberline Sea. Nestled at the head of the bay like a glowing jewel stood the Port of Shayenir.

Raure's insight had proven instrumental in Tannah's practice. Though none of them had experience with magic through the lens of a mage, nor any idea of how to provide instruction in its application, their unorthodox lessons had borne some fruit. Tannah had been able to hit her mark at fifteen paces with growing consistency; it was a small start, but it was progress all the same.

Brandt once again plunged his sword into the ground. "Tonight will be a little different." He took a few steps to the right of the sword and unsheathed the claymore from his back, burying it in the ground as well before making his way to the left an equal distance and doing the same with his skinning knife.

"This is to simulate flanking enemies. You're going to target each of the blades, starting with the one on your left, followed by the one on the right and, finally, the center target."

Tannah nodded and prepared. Once Brandt had put ample space between himself and the targets, she began. She lobbed a quick spark at the skinning knife, then wheeled around to throw another at the claymore, both finding their marks. As she launched the third toward the arming sword, it flew about halfway to its target before unexpectedly splitting, as if pulled by the other two blades and dissipating.

They all looked at each other.

"That's ... not exactly what I was expecting. I am not even quite sure what I was expecting. What happened?" Raure puzzled.

"I'm not sure," said Tannah. "I treated each attempt the same."

"Maybe just too many targets to try yet." Brandt mused. He started walking toward his arming sword. "Lets try removing o-HURK—" He crumpled into a convulsing heap on the ground between two of the blades as electricity began arcing wildly among them.

"Brandt!" Tannah screamed and darted toward him when Raure stopped her.

"Stay back! We don't know what's happening."

He ran to the claymore and batted it away with one of his massive leather gloves. Brandt's convulsions ceased. He lay on the ground coughing, a couple small wisps of smoke drifting from his form. Raure ran to his side, followed quickly by Tannah.

"Brandt, my friend, are you alright?"

Brandt coughed and sputtered. "I'm fine. I'm fine."

He sat up, his fur standing in jagged spikes, singed in places. They hauled him to his feet and they hurried away toward the campfire, watching cautiously as the last arcs jumped from blade to blade, eventually dwindling to nothing.

Raure let out a heavy sigh and they once more sat in silence for some time.

"Heh." Brandt let out a single little chuckle. Then another. They grew into a laugh, taking Tannah and Raure completely by surprise. They had never heard him laugh. They had never seen him offer up anything more than a smirk before. Even that was infrequent enough that it had seemed the man had no humor.

"Brandt ... ?" Tannah looked up at him with concern. He slapped one big hand on her back, unintentionally knocking the wind out of her.

"Kid, that was fantastic!" He let out another guffaw.

"But I didn't ..."

He stood up like a bolt.

"I know it's not what you were trying to do, but it was still amazing. Target practice is important, but *that* ..." he said, nodding to his blades in the distance, " ... That, we can *use*."

"Indeed." Raure let out a little chuckle of his own. "That is, of course, assuming we can figure out how."

Brandt collected his scattered blades from the ground.

"We will. If she did it once, she can do it again. For now, we should sleep. Tomorrow we will be at the Port." He cast his eyes to the city in the distance. "And I do not believe it will be a pleasant stay."

As Cendra approached the edge of the forest, she began to hear the clamor from the bustling city that was the Port of Shayenir. She found a suitable rock to sit on and relaxed her shoulders as she weighed her situation. Masses traveled in and out of the enormous gates of the city, going about their business as she watched the activity from behind the tree line. She looked down and frowned at the tattered wedding dress she wore. Blending in dressed this way would be difficult at best, but with no other options she would have to hope her bizarre appearance would go unnoticed in the bustle of the crowds. She brushed her hair down in front of her scales and walked briskly to the road, falling in close behind a horse and cart. Strangers cast her occasional sideways glances in her periphery, but fortunately were too preoccupied to concern themselves with her for more than a fleeting moment, allowing her to navigate the streets relatively unseen. Hunger gnawed viciously at her as she found herself outside of a bakery. She made her way inside.

Still looking down at the tray of trillhoney tarts he had been setting out, the baker welcomed her in with what seemed to Cendra's ear to be a rehearsed greeting.

"Welcome to Pranold's Pastries, sweet tooth itchin'?"

"Biscuits, I suppose—anything that would be good on the road." Cendra was keeping her face down, running her fingers through her hair to be sure it was still in front of her Scar.

"Oh, poppet! That must have been some wedding!" The man had finally taken notice of Cendra in her ruined gown. He snorted, trying to stifle his laugh as he took in her disheveled visage. "Is everything alright?"

Cendra blushed. Her voice caught in her throat as she tried to explain, but the whole truth of it was too dangerous to share. She could not afford to invite questions.

"It was a nice enough wedding, it just wasn't for me."

"Ah, I see. Say no more, love. I'll put together the 'Runaway Bride' pack for you. Where are you off to, then?"

"I ... I'm not ... " Cendra decided it was not worth arguing. "I'm looking for my friend."

"Oh. Is your friend meant to be here, then? Perhaps a customer, someone I know? What are they called?"

"Oh no, not here specifically, she is in ... Torvii Square?" Her voice bent into a question. It was clear to the baker that she had no inkling of where she was heading.

"Torvii Square?! Why would they want to meet there? It's in the heart of the Hex! There is no one there but ..." His words dropped off as he tilted his head and squinted his eyes.

The scales did not escape his scrutiny, glinting in the light behind her hair. His face went slack and he jerked backward, away from the counter, away from her. The masquerade was over—she had been seen for what she truly was. Her heartbeat became rapid as she turned on her heels and fled out the door, racing into the crowded street.

Fear gripped her as she meandered through the crowds. Though the people continued to ignore her presence, the encounter with the baker had made plain the danger she found herself in. Every passing stranger now proved a potential threat, for if any one among them took notice of her affliction they could become hostile in an instant. In this unfamiliar city, adrift in a crowd that could turn on her at any moment, Cendra had never felt so utterly scared and alone.

Overwhelmed by dread and in dire need of escape, Cendra ducked into the first vacant alley she could find. The throngs of people were not merely a threat to her; her presence was a grave danger to them. In her heart she feared that her turmoil would manifest once more in a violent flame—a flame that might consume any soul unfortunate enough to be near when she lost control.

She lingered in the alley for some time, hearing no commotion beyond the chatter of the people doing business at the shops and market stalls along the streets. To her relief, the baker must have been content just to have her leave his shop, as he had not come rushing out to warn those outside of the presence of a Scarbearer. Calm settled back into her mind as she watched them going about their carefree lives, lives not unlike the one that was hers until a few short days ago. Her stomach rumbled loudly once more—hunger demanded that she try her luck again. Satisfied that her hair was covering her scar, she left the alley hoping to find some sort of map of the city to find her way.

She walked up and down the street checking post boards and signs, but found nothing to lead her to her destination. She did, however, happen upon a street vendor selling breads and smoked meats. The pit in her stomach swelled ravenously as she neared the cart.

"What are you hungry for, miss?" The vendor's eyes were as busy as her hands, too busy to notice the crimson scales hidden behind Cendra's hair. Her disquiet eased.

"A small sourdough loaf and a link of sausage, please."

"Certainly, miss. That will be three Ilonas, if you don't mind."

The vendor turned briskly to bundle her order. She opened her mouth to ask again about the square but stopped short. To ask directly would only invite another confrontation—she would need to choose her words cautiously.

"I've never been to the city before; I'm trying to find work and a place to live, but I'm alone and don't know anyone here. Do you happen to have any suggestions where I might look, or at least where not to?"

"Well, you'd probably do well in most places. It's not a bad city. Northside's posh and full of hoity-toities." The vendor glanced at Cendra's ragged gown. "Probably not for you. I'd stay away from Stone Row at the south end of the docks if I was alone and didn't know anyone there. Further south beyond that is the Hex—keep yourself out of there." she leaned in toward her and half whispered, "Marred down there, you know."

"Marred...?"

"Yeah, marred. Scarbearers."

Cendra feigned a small gasp. "Scarbearers in the *city*? They're not exiles?"

"Well, in a manner of speaking. Not allowed outside the district, and most aren't from around here. The licensor for Quiets is down there, so marred from all around wind up there at some point. Just keep yourself out of the south end and you'll be all smiles."

"Thank you so much." Cendra handed the woman three silvers and a further three coppers for the help. She took her food and set off.

"Miss!" The vendor called after Cendra. "That's south you are headed. Keep going that way and you'll find yourself face to face with a mar."

Cendra turned and looked around, gesturing as if to use landmarks to get her bearings. She smiled and nodded, waving to the vendor.

"Thank you!"

Cendra vanished once more into the crowd. She continued west past two streets until she was sure the vendor was no longer paying any attention and turned south on the third toward the Hex.

"Fool girl. Be dead in a week," the vendor muttered to herself as she shook her head and hung the chain of sausage back on its hook.

Cendra cut a meandering path through the alleys and streets of the Port of Shayenir. After several minutes of walking, ducking in and out of passing crowds, she neared her destination. The anxiety Cendra had felt in the streets after fleeing the bakery paled in comparison to the dread she felt once she had finally set foot in the Hex. Cendra had never been face-to-face with a Scarbearer in all her days. Now, before her, dozens milled about the square. They came in all forms: short to tall, narrow to wide, young to old. Their Scars ranged from the subtle—light patches of fur, scales, or feathers—to the extreme—cloven hooves and tusks, vibrant scaled hides, tails, claws, and fangs. Her heart lurched into her throat—she feared them. Indeed, she had been raised to, they were dangerous strangers tainted by volatile magics borne of wild monsters. That old, ever-present fear was now joined by a new one: a fear that these rejected people would reject her in kind.

Curiosity and puzzlement overtook her fears as she watched from the edge of Torvii Square. The image she'd had in her mind of what she would find in the Hex stood at stark contrast to reality. The bloodthirsty monsters she had expected to find here were not skulking in the shadows. No blood in the streets, no hate in their eyes. No, they simply went about their business, much as the people outside of the Hex had. They chatted amongst themselves in small groups, toiled in surprisingly well-maintained buildings and gardens, and shopped at little market stalls some had set up around the square. She shrank as an impossibly tall figure passed close in front of her. A giant of a man trudged past, the mammoth trunk that hung from his face clutching an apple. The ground rumbled gently under her feet as he passed. He had not even registered her existence. Cendra sighed with relief. She was unremarkable here.

While she no longer had to fear that her Scar would be seen, she remained at a loss for how to find someone she did not know in a sea of strangers. Cendra found a bench situated by the tall fountain in the center of the square and sat to consider her situation. Mere moments passed before the bench groaned and sagged as a woman sat beside her. She was of early middle age; streaks of gray wove through her auburn locks with hints of wrinkles peeking from behind the headband wrapped around her forehead. While the woman who sat next to her was muscular and of stout build, she was certainly not large enough to evoke such a reaction from the bench, had it not been for her oversized arms—arms of dark stone, reminiscent of basalt. Cendra puzzled at how they could possibly move and flex, but they seemed to move with the ease of flesh. Her legs were large, as well, but Cendra could only assume they were stone as they were covered by brown rawhide pants.

"Well, child, it seems to me that the first thing we need to do is get you to the clothier, as it appears you've already found some food."

Cendra was startled, not expecting anyone to talk to her. She stared back in silence.

"You are Cendra, are you not?"

"Fionna? How did you find me?"

Fionna smirked and gestured with a large stone hand to Cendra's ruined gown.

"Well, look at you. You stand out. Even here, you stand out. Come on, let's go get you some clothes and supplies. We have a lot of work ahead of us."

CHAPTER 5
THE HOLE IN THE HEART

"I apologize, Helene, I was told I had a visitor. Had I known it was you, I would have cut my meeting short. Please come in."

Alderman Breoghan was standing in the door motioning to Helene to enter. His tall and slender frame was well-appointed in finely tailored garments dyed with dark grays and blacks. He had a stern face but his expression was kind. This gave him the appearance of someone who was pleasant and comforting, but was to be taken seriously. His look fit his demeanor and, for that matter, his position as an Alderman of the Conclave.

"There was no need, Alderman. I had my book and was perfectly content to wait." Helene replied as she stood.

"Helene, please, my name is Aethan, there is no need to be so formal."

Helene nodded and smiled as she walked through the door.

"Have a seat," Breoghan said, gesturing to an ornately carved wood and leather chair as he walked around his desk to his own. "What can I do for you?"

"Thank you. It's about Cendra…"

"Yes, of course. My sincerest apologies. I had heard about the unfortunate events at the wedding. How are you holding up? Have you been able to speak to Cendra? Is she well?"

"I am still quite shaken. I haven't been in contact with Cendra. I know she's a strong and resilient young woman, but I can't help but fear for her. She's barely ever left the walls of Esterby, and now she is out there on her own. Is there anything the Conclave can do to give her protection so she can come back?" Tears welled in Helene's eyes as she spoke.

Breoghan recognized her pain. He stood up and came around the desk to comfort her. Taking a knee by her side, he put his arm on her shoulder.

"I won't lie to you, Helene. The fear in town is at a fever pitch. This Conclave will be difficult to move to action in support of Cendra right now. I will do everything I can, though, and believe me, somehow you and I will ensure this all ends well."

Helene wiped her eyes and put her hand on Breoghan's as she stood.

"Thank you, Alder … Thank you, Aethan. Anything you can do is truly appreciated. Has there been any talk of the release of her inheritance? She will have need of it now more than ever."

"Well, this nasty business has certainly complicated matters. There has been no discussion of it within the Conclave so far. I do happen to have a thought, however—perhaps we can use this situation to hasten the release of Cendra's money. Nothing moves people to action quite like fear does. Leave it to me, Helene. I will see that the matter is addressed." He stood and shook her hand, "May I see you out?"

"Oh, no thank you. I can see my way. You are a busy man. I'll leave you to your work. Again, thank you so much ... " she hesitated slightly, " ... Aethan."

Helene made her way down Market street, taking nearly the same route through the merchant district that she and Cendra had made only days before. This time though, Helene held her head high out of spite. She could hear the mumbling onlookers as she passed. She knew the kind of gossip that was being spread by the likes of Orla and Gareth.

It made her blood boil to think of the awful things they were saying about Cendra. She had become a villain despite having done absolutely nothing wrong. She had, in fact, been a victim. Cendra would never do anything to hurt anyone. How ignorant these people were, and willfully so. How pitiful to be so cowardly that comfort could only be found by burying yourself deep in your own fear. Helene had to remind herself that the only way to fight that kind of cowardice was to model courage, to show people what it looks like to conquer fear by trying to understand the object of your fear. She hoped to find the strength to ex-emplify that model now. Helene was lost in this line of thought when a hand grabbed her shoulder. She spun around, raising her hands defensively.

"Whoa! I yield! I yield!" Abbot Larkin chuckled with his hands raised in surrender. "I'm sorry, I did not mean to startle you."

"Oh Abbot! You scared me near to death!" Helene exhaled sharply, relaxing her shoulders.

"I was just going to ask if I could walk with you for a while."

"Yes, Abbot, please do." She glanced around, frowning at the chattering masses. "I welcome any friendly company I can get right now."

Larkin joined her, staying in step with her on her right, as she walked.

"How are you holding up?" he asked.

"I'll be fine. My concern is for Cendra."

"Has there been no word yet?"

"None so far. What could take so long? Do you think something has happened?"

"Of course not. She's been gone for four days. There would be another full day before she could be expected to reach the Port of Shayenir.

It's far too early for worry—I have faith that Cendra is well."

Larkin stepped behind Helene in a quick motion to switch over to her left side, apparently allowing more room for people to pass by. It seemed odd to Helene—there had been plenty of space.

"I know. It just feels like an eternity; I have never gone more than two days without seeing her, and even then she was still in Esterby. She's never been more than a short walk beyond the gates."

As she spoke, Larkin moved back to her right side. He moved smoothly, naturally enough that Helene probably would have thought nothing of it had she not been on edge. She looked up at him and saw him glance across the street. Following his eyeline, she saw that he had looked at a group of people standing in front of the butcher's shop. She stared at them, trying to guess their connection to him. They did not appear to be anybody that Larkin would be trying to avoid for any reason.

"What are you doing?" Helene asked.

"They need to see," he replied as he smiled and waved at the onlookers.

Helene's gaze was fixed on the group, "See what?"

"That you can be treated as you always have, and that you will reciprocate in kind."

"Stop it! You look ridiculous, and all they see is you treating me differently."

"I suppose you are right. I apologize." Larkin looked back at Helene. "Helene, You look tired. Have you been eating? Let me buy you lunch. Layana is running a special on those brisket pockets."

Helene's stomach growled audibly. Layana's brisket pockets were famous. She used a sweet spicy rub on the brisket that was a well-kept secret, even from her employees. It was hickory smoked, then packed into a croissant-style dough with caramelized onions, peppers, and gruyere cheese, and cooked to flaky golden perfection.

"Oh that sounds so good, I'm afraid it would be a waste, though. I haven't had the stomach to eat since the wedding."

"You'll have to eat something, and it seems to me if something can break a fast, it's those pockets. Let's go. If you can't eat, you can take it home."

Helene could smell the brisket before they even walked in the door. She knew instantly that she would be able to eat. Her mouth was watering. They were greeted at the door by Layana, who paused for a moment when she saw Helene, but, after a look from the abbot, she smiled and led them to a table tucked into the corner. Along the way she could hear gasps and mumbling from many of the patrons.

Helene recognized what was going on right away, but did not begrudge Layana a little damage control. She could have easily refused Helene service. Larkin's eyes showed his disappointment, though.

"Do you have a table closer to the front?" he asked, giving Layana a weighted look.

"Oh, sure, I'm so sorry!" She flustered, obviously embarrassed.

"This table is just fine, Layana, thank you so much." Helene knew why the abbot was disappointed, and understood, but she did not want to have attention right now. She knew she would have to start making her presence more obvious to gain acceptance, but at this moment she was too tired and hungry to concern herself with appearances.

Layana knelt beside the table and put her hand on Helene's, "You can have whatever open seat you like, any time you come in. The abbot and I had discussed this before and I admit I faltered. Forgive me."

"It's fine, Layana, really. I am more comfortable right here, for now."

"Alright. What can I get you?"

"I think we are both wanting the special," Larkin said, as he looked at Helene for verification.

"Definitely," Helene agreed, "They smell so good. Oh, and your chilled sweetleaf tea, please."

"That sounds spectacular. I'll have the same," Larkin chimed in.

Layana smiled and stood. "Right away," she said, and left for the kitchen.

"Thank you, Abbot." Helene said apologetically, "I understand what you are trying to do, but I'll need some time before I'm ready to push back."

"I understand, I was rushing you. I'll ease off, " he said leaning back in his seat. His eyes then sharpened, and focused on hers, "but it will have to happen soon."

She nodded in agreement.

They sat in loaded silence for a few moments before Larkin spoke, "Tell me about Fionna."

Helene fidgeted with her silverware for a moment, considering what it was Larkin might want to know, what it was he needed to know, and what she needed to keep hidden. She had felt unsafe since learning the little Fionna had told her, and she did not want to put that on the abbot. Her thoughts went back to the funeral, Fionna's divulgence, and the promise Helene had made to her.

Helene's attempts to pacify Cendra were in vain and her crying was causing a distraction. She was loath to pull Cendra from her own parents' funeral, but there was no other option. She stood and, carrying a wailing Cendra, walked from her spot at the front pew toward the door. Along the way, she got sympathetic looks from those she made eye contact with. They all understood the difficult situation she was in, having been thrust into the position of caretaker in such an unexpected way while also bearing her grief. Barrett and Shyla Faraday had been her dearest friends.

Exiting the abbey, she took a seat on the stone steps. She was still trying to calm Cendra and maintain her own faltering composure when the door opened behind her. Through the door stepped Fionna, who she had come to know over the last few years through Barrett and Shyla. The Faradays had taken a trip three years prior; Fionna watched over their place while they were away. After that, she had become a fairly regular visitor, staying for weeks at a time. Over the years, Fionna and Helene had grown from acquaintances to friends by association, and on to friends in their own right.

"You're doing very well," Fionna reassured Helene as she took a seat beside her.

"I don't know what I'm doing." Helene's voice cracked as she spoke. She inhaled sharply, but released it slowly. "I'm barely keeping it together myself, and here I am trying to keep it together for her, too. I can't fathom what they were thinking of, putting me in their will."

"I know exactly what they were thinking. You have a good heart, and you are strong. You can't see it, but everyone around you can. They saw it every day, and respected you so much. You were their closest friend. Nobody could care for their child better than you. They made the perfect choice."

Fionna stood and looked seriously at her friend.

"Helene, I need you to make me a promise. I need you to swear you will see this to the end. We need to meet tonight after all of this. There are things you don't know about Cendra's family and I. Things that make it very important that she is cared for and protected. I know it's not fair to reveal all of this to you right now, but I don't have a choice. I need to leave tomorrow to take care of some things that have come to light since they passed. Promise me that you will keep her safe. In return, I will promise to help as much as I can."

"Helene?" The abbot's voice brought Helene back out of her memory. "Are you alright?"

"I'm fine, I was just thinking of Cendra." She hadn't lied. She was always thinking of Cendra, but she could not tell anyone what she knew about Cendra's parents and Fionna. "What was the question? Oh yes, Fionna. Well, she was a friend of Cendra's parents. We knew each other through them. After their funeral, she let me know that she is a Scarbearer, and that Cendra's parents were aware of it. It all had something to do with the work they did together. I don't know much more about that, or her Scar, but we have kept in contact through the years. She has visited many times to check in on Cendra. The visits were always a secret, even to Cendra; they had to be for both of their safety. When this Scarbearer mess started, she was my first thought."

"Ha! Scarbearer in town, right under our noses!" The abbott sat back and let out a chuckle. "Gareth would lose his mind to hear this."

Larkin leaned forward, rubbing his hands together, practically licking his chops at the thought of Gareth's face if he found out. He looked up at Helene and composed himself instantly. "Oh! Of course I'd never tell him, but you must admit, the thought is humorous."

They both had a healthy laugh. Helene realized how grateful she was to have run into Larkin; it had been the first laugh she'd had since the wedding. It had been desperately needed, far more than she had known.

"Thank you, Abbott, I needed that."

"As did I, Helene. You couldn't know how much." He let out another small chuckle, remembering the thought of Gareth's face, and let it fade, smiling back at Helene. "Thank you."

Layana returned with the brisket pastries. They were golden brown, fresh from the wood-fired oven. The abbot had barely finished the blessing when Helene ripped hers open and took a large bite. The pastry was flaky and moist. The brisket fell apart in her mouth with sauce and cheese coming together perfectly. Helene had found her appetite.

The design of the Esterby Abbey was in stark contrast to that of the town itself. Opulent and domineering, it loomed over the town like a giant. Fluted limestone pillars supported the massive roof and ornate gargoyles. Inside, the long chamber was lined on either side by white marble towers, carved likenesses of former honored alderpersons, standing on the glossy onyx floor; they held the ceiling overhead. At the east end, three gilded thrones stood atop a stage.

Every step echoed throughout the empty hall as Helene and the abbot entered. The Conclave meeting would not start for nearly thirty minutes, but Breoghan had asked them to see him beforehand. They stood together in front of the Pillar of Thoerne, admiring the craftsmanship, while they waited.

"Erasmus Thoerne. He was the founder of Esterby, and an original member of the Conclave,"

Breoghan said as he joined them. "He fought with Protector Regent Shayenir, in the War of Silence."

"The War of Silence?" The abbot laughed, "A fairy tale, is it not? I have not heard anyone speak of it beyond nursery rhymes, and ancient folk songs."

"It is no mere fairy tale. It happened, though memory of it has faded, lost and forgotten to time."

"Yet, here you are telling us of the people who fought in it." The doubt in Helene's voice had a ring of mockery.

"One of my peculiarities, I suppose," the alderman chuckled, "In my idle time I look for ancient knowledge, and historical texts. I have a passion for history, but please, do not let me bore you with my hobbies. We have more pertinent topics to discuss." Seeing people entering the hall, Alderman Breoghan motioned toward his chamber, "A little more privacy is warranted, I believe."

Following them into his chamber, Breoghan closed the door behind him.

"Now, Helene, I just had a few things to discuss before the meeting. First is just a little housekeeping for the Conclave. I'm trying to get them to approve the release of Cendra's inheritance. First, I need you to confirm these numbers."

He handed Helene a parchment.

"I think this all looks correct," she affirmed after looking over the figures.

"Excellent. They have also asked me about a discrepancy in the inventory of her belongings. It seems there is an item missing from your original list. A pendant, I believe." He shuffled through his papers, "Yes, it says here that the item in question is a red, faceted pendant on a chain. It appears to be absent from storage."

Helene tilted her head in confusion. "Is it really that big of a concern? It's just a bauble."

"I'm afraid the other Alderpersons are being very particular."

"Well, she has it with her. She has always had it. It seemed like a personal item, not important enough to worry about."

Breoghan took a deep breath, "So she has it with her even now?"

"Yes, she would never let it go. Why is this such a concern?" Helene was getting worried now.

"I'll be honest, the rest of the Conclave is fighting against me on this. I believe they will use any discrepancy, no matter how insignificant it may seem, to deny Cendra's claim." He walked back to his door, opened it, and glanced around out in the hall. He then shut the door again, and returned to his desk. He leaned in close and spoke quietly. "I was afraid that she would have it, so I've had this made." He produced a tear-shaped glass pendant on a chain. "Turn this in as the item.

That will close that question, and will give us a better chance."

"I don't think she—" The abbot started to object, but was cut off by Breoghan.

"Are we going to let them deny Cendra her money for a bauble? This is the weapon they have, and they will use it. She's going to lose everything, Helene."

Helene looked to the abbot, hoping for a better option. He thought for a time, but, coming up with nothing, he threw his hands in the air.

Helene exhaled sharply, "Alright, Aethan, if you think that's best."

"Marvelous! I believe that covers everything. Go on out and find your seats and leave the rest to me." Breoghan stood, and guided them to the door.

"The next item, gentlemen, is the matter of the estate of Barrett and Shyla Faraday" Breoghan was extremely formal in both attire and manner during the Conclave meeting. "Seated in the front, you will find Helene Lochart, representing their daughter, and only heir, Cendra Faraday. Having investigated the matter fully, as requested by the other members of this Conclave, it is my recommendation that we proceed with the release of the estate to Cendra, as prescribed by the Will and Testament of the deceased, and the laws of the city of Esterby."

"I do not believe it to be as simple as all of that, Alderman." Alderman Stonlek, President of the Conclave, sat in the center throne. "I did not know Cendra, I am sure that she was a fine young woman; indeed, by all accounts, she was. That does not change her current circumstances. I do not think it would be proper for this conclave to fund a Scarbearer. Think of the damage that money could cause."

"You speak, sir, as if the money in question belongs to the Conclave," countered Alderman Breoghan. "We are merely the temporary stewards of Cendra's inheritance. To deny her inheritance is counter to the laws of Esterby, and the honor of this Conclave. In case you have forgotten, there was nearly a riot in the streets when this Conclave appointed itself conservators of the estate, which I voted against. May I also remind you that you almost lost your position on the Conclave over it?"

"What is right is often not popular, Alderman. We did what needed to be done, and thank the gods for it. This money should not find its way into the hands of those in the thrall of magic. I move that the funds be immediately released to the Conclave for special projects as deemed necessary by the Conclave—the first of which will be a monument to the memory of Barrett and Shyla Faraday."

Helene's gasp was immediately overpowered by the applause of the others in attendance.

Stonlek waited for the applause to die down before continuing, "If it is popularity you are concerned about, Breoghan, I think you will find that the people of Esterby will support us in this matter."

"What is right is often not popular, Alderman."

CHAPTER 6

THE FURY IN THE FLAME

Fionna had a small residence just outside of the Port of Shayenir, a short walk south of the Hex. Older, but well maintained, the house was well-organized and decorated with many pieces of old art and antiques. It was close enough to the city for easy access to goods and sundries, but far enough to afford a small amount of privacy. Though small, there was a spare room with a bed. Cendra was thankful to have a comfortable place to sleep; she felt she had so little left to be thankful for.

For nigh on three weeks, Fionna had been trying to help Cendra gain some control over the flame of her Scar with no progress to show for their efforts. The pace had proved frustratingly slow. This morning, as with every morning before, Fionna had taken Cendra behind the house for training. Fionna had set up a fire pit some distance from her house—the intent was for Cendra to light it, but so far they had been met with only failure. Fionna had begun to question Cendra's account of the fire in the forest, and indeed whether any powers had manifested at all.

"Are you certain that you were the cause of the fire? Think back. Could it have been an existing fire that had gotten out of control, or some unseen beast? Or perhaps you dreamt it?"

"I *know*," Cendra huffed. "It wasn't a dream. I could feel the flame leaving my body as I collapsed, and when I awoke the forest was scorched." Cendra's mounting frustration bled into her tone.

"I'm sorry, it's just that we've seen no evidence of flame of any sort. I can see the Scar clearly, but something should be manifesting. It just isn't." Fionna sighed and shook her head. "Let's take a little break."

"Good, I'm done for a while." Cendra was not about to argue. They had been at it all morning. She had grown hungry and irritable; she was on the edge of an eruption and she knew it. She felt it better to stop and relax for a while, for who could tell what damage she might cause.

In the kitchen, Fionna checked the crooner shrimp and wild rice dish she had made up and hung over the coals. She spooned a sample in her mouth and then added some seasonings from her pantry. After giving it a stir, she filled a small bowl and set it on the table in front of Cendra.

"Thank you" Cendra barely got the words out before shoveling a spoonful to her mouth. She missed her mom's cooking, but had been enjoying Fionna's more worldly dishes. "Are you not eating?"

Helene sat at her writing desk, and took up an iridescent green perryton quill. "I'm not hungry right now."

"What are you doing?"

"I'm answering that letter I received from Helene yesterday. You should answer yours, as well."

"I wrote to her last night. It's there in the last cubby in your desk," she looked up from her bowl to see Fionna smiling at her. "What?"

"You look like your father, but you eat like your mother," Fionna laughed.

Cendra was taken aback. Fionna had not mentioned her parents once, the entire time she had been there. She knew Fionna had known her parents and had wanted to ask questions, to learn more about them. However, not knowing their relationship, she had wanted to let Fionna broach the subject. After the first week passed with no mention of them, Cendra had assumed her parents were an uncomfortable subject for the woman. It was probably best to leave it alone, at least until she knew Fionna better. To hear her suddenly bring them up so casually and cheerfully seemed odd, but now that the opportunity had presented itself, she pressed.

"How did you know them?" Cendra put her spoon down and leaned back in her chair, getting comfortable for what she hoped would be a long conversation.

Fionna's smile faded as she fidgeted with her quill.

"I worked with them. Surely Helene told you."

"She didn't tell me much at all. I knew of you. I knew you were an old friend of my parents. I didn't know you were a Scarbearer, or really anything else for that matter."

"There really isn't much else to tell. We worked together," Fionna stood and took Cendra's bowl and spoon back into the kitchen.

Cendra followed her, "Doing what?"

"Oh nothing exciting. We were antiquarians, I guess you would say." Fionna gestured to the antiques that decorated her place. "We sought and acquired rarified antiques, to preserve the past."

Cendra picked up a small brass balance scale sitting on the counter. "Is this stuff really that important? My parents made a living off of this?"

Fionna glanced back from the hearth, after having placed the empty bowl and spoon into the pot of hot water above the fire. She quickly moved over to her and took the scales.

"Sorry, dear, these are very, ummm, fragile. One must be careful not to touch any of these antiques. Maybe we should get back to training."

Cendra grunted in frustration. "Why? It's useless. I'm sick of even trying." She returned to her chair and flopped down gracelessly.

"I understand that, but it really is important that we keep trying," Fionna carefully placed the balance scales back down on the counter. "You have the mark now, there is no hiding it. So, if you are to survive out there, you will need to develop and hone these skills ... whatever they are. Society holds a capricious dichotomy for Scarbearers. Our value to the outside world lies in the very magic they have shunned us for. It's a shame, it really is, they hate us for it, so we are useless to them until they need it. Wrong or right, it's the way of the world, if you want to survive, you need to play along."

Though she hid it well, Cendra's blood boiled to think of being treated this way, to be cast aside as if she were garbage, and then called on to help when magic was needed. She stewed over the thought as Fionna led her outside to the fire pit.

"Remember to concentrate. Imagine the logs on fire. Picture it in your mind and focus upon it."

Fionna wished there was a true discipline involved, a tangible set of steps in the training of a Scarbearer. The reality was more complex; Scarbearers with an elemental affinity had to find the trigger for their gifts. All she could do was to help Cendra to focus, prod her to try harder when she lost will, and recognize their breakthroughs—if any were to be had. She had trained some Scarbearers in her time, but never had she seen one struggle so hard to draw out their power.

Fionna's frustration paled in comparison to Cendra's. She had been at it for weeks, going through the motions for Fionna, trying to train to be something she did not want to be in the first place. To help people that thought her less than human. It was all so unfair. She threw her arms up, exasperated.

"I can't do it!"

"Of course you can. You just need to concentrate."

"I swear, Fionna, I can't hear you say that again! You're meant to be training me, and all you've had me do is stare at an unlit campfire and yell 'Concentrate!' at me for weeks! By the Triune, if I hear the word 'concentrate' one more time ..." she let the sentence end there.

"I understand. I'm frustrated too. This truly is the first step. You must be able to call the power intentionally to start to understand how to gain control of it. We must keep trying. Just look at it and conc–" Fionna caught Cendra's glare and corrected herself " —think really hard."

Cendra did as instructed, but not without obvious, though silent, protest and annoyance. Sitting down, she faced the neatly stacked kindling and logs, furrowed her brow and stared at it. She tried to direct her anger at it—this was mostly out of her frustration over the situation, but it also made sense to her that if she wanted something to burn she should hate it. She soon became acutely aware of Fionna's intense observation. Cendra seethed—now trying less to set logs on fire than trying *not* to set Fionna on fire.

The following hour crawled for Fionna. She paced back and forth endlessly, the plod of her feet grating on Cendra's ears. She noticed Cendra's head slightly reacting to her movements. "Stop following me and what I'm doing, you need to conc–" With a great roar, the fire pit and everything surrounding it was engulfed in white hot flame.

Cendra sat once more in the crackling aftermath, tormented by fear of what she would see when she opened her eyes. What she feared most since the night in the woods had finally come to pass—she had incinerated someone alive. She sat weeping for a moment that felt endless.

"What in the Hells?!"

She opened her eyes to find a bewildered, yet curiously unharmed Fionna staring at her, wide-eyed, her clothes still aflame.

A further three weeks had passed since Cendra first lashed out at Fionna, but merely a day had passed since the last. Fionna began to feel overwhelmed, and her frustration compounded Cendra's own. She had given Cendra a day to relax, something she had taken to doing every other day. The girl was in desperate need of the rest, but so was Fionna. Doubt had emerged: doubt that she could continue Cendra's training—if what they had done in the last several weeks could be called that. Proper training could not begin until she knew what she was dealing with.

Concerns weighed heavy on Fionna's mind. Even after these weeks spent together, still all that was known is what she had learned from talking to Cendra on that first day with one major exception—she had seen firsthand how terribly powerful and volatile she was. This became more apparent with each day spent in the yard on their ineffectual exercises until Cendra's patience shattered—each outburst more devastating than the last. Too much remained unknown about the nature of Cendra's Scar. It was clear to Fionna that Cendra's Scar was bestowed upon her when she was too young to remember, and there was no doubt that it was related to the fire that claimed her parents. Nothing she had learned in this time gave any indication of what kind of monster could have bestowed the Scar, nor how Cendra had survived the encounter.

Fionna needed information. A visit to Porter in Stone Row was in order, but her need was vague—it would be a big ask. If anyone could get information, or find a person to help, it would be Porter. Fionna needed an excuse to get away from home, anyway. She could tell Cendra was feeling cooped up, too. A couple of days away from the house might help reset, even if it was just in Stone Row. They would go see Porter tomorrow—assuming they did not kill each other first.

Cendra sat alone in the backyard. The weeks of training had taken a toll. She was tired, angry, and homesick. She wanted to see her mother—but far beyond that, she desperately wanted to turn back time to before all of this.

"I'd give anything ..." Cendra could not help but speak it out loud to the empty air, or perhaps to the Sisters. Maybe they'd hear and have some mercy. "... to sleep in my own bed. Hot chicory and ambercane with Mom in the morning. Even to just chat again with Orla and Layana in the market. ..."

"The same Orla that would as soon see you dead now?

She was startled by Fionna's voice, who had approached behind as she voiced her wish to no one. "... It's not Orla in particular that I want to go back to."

"What you miss is knowing your place in the world. Acceptance. Routine. Comfort."

"Something like that."

"Would it help to know that all of that is attainable again? You have a new life now—there are no two ways about it. But that does not mean that you can't get comfortable with it, or that you can't find your place in the world."

They sat in silence, as Cendra considered the thought. For the first time she let the truth wash over her—and with it, a wave of calm. She lifted her eyes to the pile of wood. With a deep breath, she imagined a flame, a flame like the little candle in her Rumination. As they sat silently, a little waft of smoke began to drift up from the wood as it slowly started to glow. The glow quickly ignited into a roaring flame. She looked to Fionna, who jumped to her feet.

"My word, Child. ... you've done it!" Fionna glanced quickly around the yard and selected a small twig from the ground. "Can you do it again?"

Cendra smiled and nodded. "I think so!"

Fionna threw the little stick out before them—this time, Cendra set it ablaze almost instantly. They grabbed each other by the shoulders, jumping and laughing excitedly.

"Hold on, I'll be right back!" Fionna ran into the cabin and came back out with a bottle. "I would say we certainly have something to celebrate!" She filled a pair of mugs and handed one to Cendra.

Cendra grabbed the mug eagerly. She had not been allowed alcohol yet. This would be her first taste, and what a perfect moment for it.

"What is it?" she asked, sniffing the deep blue liquid.

"It's dawnberry wine—I brewed it myself from dawnberries of those very vines over there."

"You made this?"

"Yes, it's from my fourth year out here. I had just hit my stride learning to make wine, and it happened to be a great year for the berries. I save this vintage for special occasions."

Cendra smiled and tipped the mug toward Fionna before bringing it to her lips for her first taste. It was very sweet, with a deep floral flavor and a bright finish.

"It's delicious!" She exclaimed, tipping back another drink.

"You don't have to act so surprised. ... and slow down! It's deceptively strong. It sneaks up even on experienced drinkers."

Cendra blushed and set her mug to the side to show that she understood. "You have a lot of hidden talents, don't you?"

"What do you mean?"

"Well, you make great wine, you train the untrainable, and you... you... what? You can block fire?"

"I was wondering when you'd finally ask. No, I can't block anything. I have a very high tolerance to heat, pain, impacts, among other things. Some call Scarbearers of my nature earthmovers, quakers, or rockies. Technically I'm Golemkind—got pinched by a boulderclaw. ..." She saw by Cendra's expression that she was having difficulty keeping up; life in Esterby had kept her sheltered from knowledge of most things in the world of Scarbearers. Fionna slowed down. "A stone scorpion. It was a moment of ignorance, and it forever changed me—for better or worse."

"Better?" Cendra was surprised by that word. How could being a Scarbearer possibly make her life better?

"Oh, I suppose I am to live the rest of my life mourning my past life. Scarbearers are a scourge. They are hated by everyone, not least of all themselves. Am I right?"

"I did not mean to offend you, and I didn't think that. ... Exactly."

"I don't offend easily, dear. Thick skin and all. I know what you meant. I went through everything you are going through, years ago. Time is the most powerful magic of all. It wears down mountains. It softens the edges of our pain. Most importantly, though, it teaches. I've had a very long and thorough education. I've seen good in Scarbearers and norms alike, and the same goes for evil. No one is devoid of either. Certainly Helene has taught you as much."

Cendra considered that. Of course she had heard that many times from her mother, why had it not set in with her in regard to Scarbearers?

"Oh yes. Many times. I'm embarrassed to say, though, that she had only one voice, and there are many in Esterby. Hers carried immeasurable weight with me. But I'm afraid that the others may have done a job of drowning her out somewhat." She wiped a tear, fully feeling the shame of disappointing her mother.

"Dear Cendra, don't dwell on that. That is the curse of all parents. You are no different. Helene knows that. She is a daughter herself, you know." Fionna smiled at her and took a sip of wine, leaning back in her seat, relaxing to fully enjoy the drink.

Cendra sat back too, leaning up quickly after to fetch her forgotten mug. She took a sip, and leaned back again. Thoughts of home and her mother filled her mind while they sat quietly for a time.

"How ... How do you know Mom?" Cendra interrupted the conversational hiatus with a question that was meant to be silent, but came out unexpectedly.

"I met her through your parents." Fionna hesitated. She was not sure how much Helene had shared with Cendra about her parents. Reading no distress on Cendra's face, she continued, "I worked with your parents. Helene and I ran into each other many times. We have kept in touch since their passing."

"Can you tell me about them?"

"What do you want to know?"

"What was the work you did together?"

Fionna looked down at her wine, swirling it around in the mug.

"We worked to find, recover, and preserve magical knowledge and artifacts." She looked up at Cendra. "Your parents were remarkable people. They put their lives on the line to save magic, because they did not believe what the world says about magic. They were not content to let fear destroy something so wonderful."

Cendra leaned forward, shaking her head with confusion.

"Were they Scarbearers too?"

"Oh no, dear, they had no magic, but they saw the beauty in it, and understood that it was a natural part of the world we live in. They were ... extraordinary people."

"Helene won't talk about the fire. I've always had this feeling that she was hiding something. Do you know why?"

"I'm sure you are reading too much into that. It is just a painful subject for anyone who knew them." Fionna stood up, finishing her wine. "We have a long day tomorrow, dear. We are going into the city to visit a friend in Stone Row who can maybe get some answers about your situation. We had better turn in."

Cendra started to protest, but quickly realized she wasn't going to get her way. She tipped back the rest of her wine and headed to bed.

CHAPTER 7

THE WOLF IN THE CITY

Water had begun finding its way through the holes in his boots. The clamor of the shabby east end of the dock district had already eaten away at Brandt's patience without the added annoyance of damp feet. Tannah and Raure, for their part, were in high spirits despite the general gloom of the soggy cobblestones and rotting wood that made up the sullen interior of the Port of Shayenir, dubbed "Stone Row" by the locals, a refuge for the outcasts of society and haven for the desperate and unscrupulous.

He let out a weighty sigh. They were in need of supplies and shelter, and almost desperately short on coin. Tannah's parents sent regular letters to her with a stipend for her care, but it would not be enough. It was clear that even though they had to send her away they still loved her dearly; but love alone would not fill stomachs, nor would it educate a temperamental young mage. However unprepared they were, they would need work very quickly.

Raure's gloved open hand made a firm impact between his shoulder blades, snapping him from his deliberations. "You are looking even more dour today than usual. An accomplishment, to be sure."

"No more dour than our situation is dire." Brandt glanced around the bustling docks. It might have been described as vibrant if all around them had not been sickly grays or browns. "We need food, supplies, shelter, work. ... I'm not even sure where to start."

"Well, the good news is that when *everything* is a priority, *nothing* is a priority," Raure chuckled. "Pick one problem and we'll start there, but a bit of wisdom my friend—problems seem smaller on a full stomach."

Cendra stayed on Fionna's heels as they worked their way past what she guessed to be over a hundred street vendors in the bustling market of Stone Row. With the exception of her short time in city limits trying to find Fionna, this was her first time in the city. Without the panic and confusion, she was able to take in the sites, the sounds, and, most notably, the smells. There were so many wonderful fragrances created by the food vendors, and they were all competing for her olfactory attention with the fishmongers, and just barely losing. She was so excited by this new experience that she was enjoying it all.

Fionna, on the other hand, was on a mission. She had spent a lot of time in Stone Row throughout the years and was no longer so enamored with the piscine-fragranced charms of the market, and had no interest in dallying about. Deftly weaving through the vendors, she led them directly to a blue door situated in a graying and worn brick storefront. Above the door hung a tattered sign which was no longer legible save for the word "Porter " She walked right in, seemingly as comfortably as walking into her own home.

She turned and greeted the receptionist, a young man with pale blue eyes that were a sharp contrast to his coal-black hair and bronze skin.

"Good morning, Greshi. Is he in?"

"Sorry, Fi. He's out today. On a job, you know. He will be back in the morning, or tonight if it is urgent."

"It can wait until the morning. Do you think there are some rooms at The Crow's Nest?"

"Certainly. It's pretty slow here today. There is a Tukfin run out near the Docelin Isles, so the boats are all out for a few days."

"Right, we'll get a room and be back in the morning. Who's serving the best food lately?"

"You have to try Capt'n T'Ristle's. They've been getting the catch of the day very regularly, and they have an amazing cook."

"Thank you. We will see you tomorrow"

Tannah stared hungrily as the leg roast, vegetables, and warm bread were set on the table between them. They had found a little cookery tucked in amongst the various stalls, shops, and warehouses lining Stone Row—perhaps only marginally less dingy than its surroundings, but the hearth was warm and it smelled only vaguely of deceased fish. The meal had set them back an Armine and a quarter, nearly a third of their remaining coin; but after such a long journey and before the obstacles they were to surmount, they were in dire need of a meal of some quality.

Brandt produced his skinning knife and began slicing the roast. "We are going to need to find paying work quickly. This little feast has significantly lightened our purse."

"Well, we cannot hunt yet," Raure opined as Tannah shoveled vegetables and sliced meat onto her plate. "We are but three; no client would consider us for a contract. We have no license and are short the hands to acquire one. That leaves us odd jobs until our situation changes."

"We'll work it out!" Tannah managed to choke out between mouthfuls.

"Hah! We will indeed." Raure couldn't help but smile.

They ate in silence for several minutes.

"It has gotten a bit late in the day for job hunting," Brandt remarked as he ripped a final hunk of bread free from the loaf. "For now we should focus on finding a place to stay and stow our belongings. That is, if we can afford it."

Tannah slouched back in her chair, full. She stifled a satisfied belch.

Throngs of people passed by them on the way to their homes as Brandt eyed the lodging postings on the billing board.

"A full Armine a night ... ?" He struggled to hide his frustration. The pittance they had on them would not even carry them to the end of the week before food. The price seemed outrageous in the squalor of Stone Row.

"It seems we have arrived at work being the priority," Raure murmured. "I suppose we could return to the chophouse and ask if they need any cookware cleaned or rats crushed. ..."

"Hey Brandt ..." Tannah tugged on his shirt. "Give me a handful of cops."

"Tannah, we do not have money to spare," he grunted.

She met his eyes. "Please ... Trust me."

Brandt let out a heavy sigh. He was her custodian for now, but it was her money in the pouch. He loosened the strap on the coin purse and shook out four copper Eduni and placed them gently in her hand. Tannah closed her hand around them and walked a few paces from her companions. She pinched one of the coins between her finger and thumb and gave it a small charge, then with her thumb deftly flipped it to her other palm. Casting it into the air above her head, she charged another coin, and another, flipping them each to her other hand and pitching it over her head after the others. As she charged each coin, they took on a gentle glow in the settling twilight; one azure, then one gold, alternating as they passed between her hands and glided over her head in a lazy arc. A handful of people passing by stopped to observe as the coins seemed to linger overhead, slowly passing through the air and gently falling back into her hand before being passed once more back into the loop.

She smiled at one of the passersby as her hands deftly worked.

"Four of them is easy. I can do more!"

The old fisherman smiled as his eyes followed the coins as they danced overhead. From his pocket he produced a silver Ilona and flicked it into the air. As it fell through the sky toward Tannah, an almost imperceptible arc popped among it and the surrounding coins and it snapped itself into the span between them, taking on a soft green glow and pushing them each away until they were once more equidistant. The fisherman clapped gleefully, mesmerized by the dancing lights as others started to gather around. From the small but growing crowd, every now and then a new coin would flip into the air to be claimed by the loop.

Brandt and Raure watched the slowly growing ballet of metal in silence. On the periphery of his vision, Raure caught a small smile creeping across Brandt's face. He wasn't watching the coins; he was watching Tannah. Raure had only seen the expression on his face in one other place: the countenance of a proud parent.

The glint of a golden Armine in the now fairly crowded loop of coins caught Tannah's eye. It was time to end the show—she did not want to take more donations from these downtrodden people than they needed to get by. To signal the finale, she gently started accelerating the loop; the coins spinning faster and faster in the air until their blur resembled a luminous wheel. With a clap, she ground the wheel to a halt, the coins hanging overhead, wobbling gently before falling to the ground like rain around her as she gave a large, flourishing bow. The little crowd applauded and cheered loudly, then slowly dispersed as Tannah began gathering the coins from the ground. The show had only lasted a few minutes, but by Brandt's estimate of the coins on the ground, she had tripled their purse in that short span of time. Raure helped Tannah gather the money as she felt Brandt's hand on her shoulder.

"Well done, kid," he said with a chuckle. "You're already far and away our most valuable asset."

Brandt and Raure woke early on the second day. Tannah's impromptu light show had afforded them enough money to secure some semblance of comfort for the night; the lodgings were quaint but the beds were dry and warm. There was no time to relax, however—they had business to attend to, and Brandt knew just who to see.

"You've mentioned a friend of yours here in the city once or twice. Presumably that is who we're visiting today?"

"'Friend' might be a strong word. More of an 'informant' of sorts." Brandt let out a little scoff. "He prefers the term 'information broker.'"

"Fair enough. What is it you hope to find?"

"He is a connection for Scarbearers. A trait we used to lean on back in the military."

Raure found the implications unpleasant and his face reflected it. Brandt continued.

"It's not as sinister as it sounds, but still, Porter's primary concern is Porter and we will leave it at that. He may have information on others we can recruit. He also usually has leads on hunts that are either too trivial or too complex for most Quiets to bother to undertake. He may have something for us, and right now we have to take what we can get."

He walked to the door to Tannah's room and opened it. "Tannah, come on. We have to go."

She rolled slightly in her bed and let out a muffled groan. "Just a bit longer."

Brandt opened his mouth to protest, but something caught in his throat and lingered. "Okay." He gently closed the door.

It was an unassuming building at the head of the docks, and much like the rest of the architecture in Stone Row it was old, gray, and weathered. The only indication of what was inside was a battered and rotted wooden sign, the top half of which was illegible, but the bottom half read "Porter." It wasn't the man's name—Brandt had never bothered to learn it—but his "official" job title, and consequently what everyone he knew called him.

The interior was a stark contrast. It was well appointed; oil lamps lit the interior with a warm amber glow. Tall, intricately carved bookcases and magnificently framed paintings of landscapes—a handful of which Brandt had seen in person—lined the far walls. Immediately inside the door, a row of simple yet well-crafted chairs waited at the entryway. A delicately woven rug of red and gold lay centered on the floor, upon which a desk sat covered in scattered parchments, open ledgers, and ink blots. Behind the reception desk, standing in a doorway to the inner office was a large man of some age, tall and of stout frame; it was a build that suggested he was shy of neither work nor meal. A pair of round, wire-frame spectacles rested on the tip of his nose, and a bushy, whiting gray beard completely obscured the lower half of his face. White hair crowned the top of his head, oiled back smoothly. The scent of the herb-infused oil assaulted Brandt's nose, heavy with imp's mint and lavender. Porter smirked as recognition set in.

"You need a shave." He paused and made an audible sniff. "And a bath. What can I do for you, Captain Brandt?"

"Smells like an alchemist's latrine in here. Where is Greshi? This place won't last too long if it's left to you."

Porter gave a wry smirk.

"That smell came in with you. Greshi is out for a moment. He'll be back soon, I think I can handle it until then. It's been some years since you've graced my office with your presence. Heard you'd had a run in with a bargy and got discharged." His eyes softened with genuine sympathy. "I am truly sorry for your lost comrades ... and your condition."

Brandt shrugged the topic aside, not eager to revisit history. "My—*our*—condition, as you put it, is why we are here. We are forming a Quiet."

Porter's eyebrows raised in intrigue. He stepped back into the doorway and ushered the group into his office. "Quite the career shift, given your history, don't you think?"

After Brandt took a seat in front of Porter's desk Porter took his place behind it. Seeing there was only one seat left, Raure stepped to the side, and motioned to Tannah to have a seat. She smiled and nodded a thank you as she sat down.

"I've not come to dig up bones, Porter. This is the only option I've got at present."

"So it would seem."

"To cut to the heart of the matter, we need a job."

"Well, I am sure we can probably find you something. If it's a new troupe you're organizing, we'll need to draw up the license first." Porter pulled an empty form from the piles on his desk and readied a quill. "Alright, one at a time, names and ages."

"Raure Irelos, thirty-five."

"Next?"

Brandt let out a heavy sigh. "Brandt Lyfir Ostenbrad Kramenberg von Lusenbil III, thirty-nine."

Tannah snorted loudly.

"Next?"

"Tannah Pyxner, fourteen."

Porter stopped writing. "... *Fourteen?*"

"Yes."

"Triune's sake, Brandt, she's just a lass! Has she ever even seen a beast?!"

Brandt shot her a glance, and she shook her head. "That'd be a no."

Porter looked Tannah over. "I don't see a Scar. Does that make her a Caller, or just particularly gifted at hopscotch?"

"I'm a Caller, and I know what I'm doing. Brandt is teaching me."

"Oh, sure, why not. I'm sure he's just the perfect instructor." Porter rubbed the bridge of his nose. "Glossing over that for now, who is next?"

Brandt paused a moment before answering. "That's it."

Porter slammed the form down on his desk. "What do you mean, 'that's it'? Ignoring the fact that your Caller is a mere child with no experience, I cannot even issue a license to a Quiet of less than four people. You'd be endangering not only yourselves, but your clients! This is a serious business for seasoned hunters, not a child and her sitters."

Tannah's eyes began to well up. A line had been crossed—Brandt's stress had surpassed its peak, and seeing Tannah hurt sent him headlong into a rage. His fangs and claws were already bared as he leapt to his feet. Quicker still was Raure, who had already interposed himself between the two, face to face with Porter, his gloved hand on Brandt's chest, holding him back.

"I will not have such a loathsome man as yourself behave in such an unseemly manner toward a young woman who has been nothing but friendly and courteous to you. You are not her superior, sir. You have proved not even her equal. You will apologize."

"You forget yourself, Scarbearer, I'm not someone you can afford to anger." Porter moved to his door and opened it, signaling that he was finished with them.

Brandt snarled as he reached past Raure and gripped Porter's lapel, jerking him in close. "Is it us that forgets, *meat*, that I could flay the flesh from your bones before your wails escaped these walls? You will treat us with ..." Brandt stopped, catching an unfamiliar but curious scent out in the waiting room. Looking past Porter he saw the source—two Scarbearers: an older lady sitting and a younger one who had just sprung to her feet, seemingly ready to fight.

He tilted his right ear up in her direction, not taking his eyes off of Porter. His hackles fell. He knew if the situation escalated further it would undoubtedly get out of hand, ruining any chance of jobs through Porter in the future if it had not already. He also had no idea what the pair in the waiting room were capable of, but could sense they were powerful. Together, they smelled of brimstone.

Fionna reached up and put her hand on Cendra's shoulder.

"Not our fight, dear," She whispered calmly, beckoning Cendra to sit.

Brandt backtracked, hoping to calm things down. He motioned to Raure and Tannah to back off.

"I apologize, Porter. We are merely desperate. We mean no disrespect."

"I understand, Brandt. I'm willing to forget this, but you have to know I can't send such a small team on a hunt with such an inexperienced Caller. I have a reputation and I need to keep that reputation if I'm not to end up penniless and desperate myself. I would recommend you for some small jobs, if you got someone, anyone with experience. Come back with another body and a better mood—or not at all." He turned to acknowledge Tannah. "Young lady, Your friends are quite right. I do owe you an apology. I mean no disrespect to you at all. In the business of hunting, inexperience can be deadly. I only meant to look out for everyone involved."

Brandt nodded and turned to leave. Getting his first real look at Fionna and Cendra, they did not look as fearsome as they smelled. He tilted his head slightly, trying to read them.

"Fionna!" Porter called, "Good to see you! Come on in."

Fionna and Cendra stood and walked toward Porter. Fionna smiled as they moved past Brandt and the others, a gesture in stark contrast to Cendra's best tough glare. This failed to elicit the reaction she had wanted from Brandt—he smirked with a snort, seeming genuinely amused.

"What can I do for you, Fionna?" Porter asked, pointing them to the chairs as he shut the door behind them.

"I'm looking for information on unusual Scarbeareres. Particularly, Scarbearers that never had the Fever, had a very mild Fever, or survived the Fever as an infant."

Porter eyed Cendra, "What's your name?"

"Cendra Faraday."

"Hello, Cendra. I'm Porter. Am I to believe that you are a Scarbearer, and have not had the Fever?"

"I'm not a Scarbearer, because I've never been attacked, and I've never had the Fever."

He folded his eyebrows at her. "But you have suddenly gained some sort of magical power, and a scale-covered Scar on your face?"

Cendra sighed heavily. She was not ready to accept her fate as a Scarbearer and could not stand to have people acting as if they knew her situation better than she did. Porter, above any of the others, had exacerbated her irritation by his nature as a know-it-all prick.

"Oh! I never looked at it like that! Thank the Triune we've come to such a wise and knowledgeable person! We can go home now." Cendra's scathingly sarcastic rant trailed off as she caught Fionna's glare. She looked down at her fists. They glowed red as if ready to burst, but Cendra felt control—she knew that she could keep the fire contained. She could hold it back—that is, if Porter kept his mouth shut.

Stepping out of Porter's door, they were met immediately by Brandt. Fionna stepped in front of Cendra, her body tensed and ready to fight, but Brandt could tell by the look in her eye that she was not looking to. He raised his hand in peace.

"I just want to talk. I have no fight with the two of you. What I do have is an offer," he said.

"What sort of offer?" Fionna asked warily.

"We need another experienced member for our team. You carry yourself like someone who has been in plenty of skirmishes."

Fionna shook her head. "I'm not interested. I have no desire for that life any more. I'm long past my prime, at any rate."

"Past your prime? From what I know about Golemkind, you are still well within it." Seeing Fionna's reaction to his accurate identification of her Scar, he explained. "Not much gets past this nose."

"Impressive," she replied. "I will grant you that there is probably still plenty of fight left in the body, but the heart and mind have seen enough."

"You don't need to fight. I'm asking for your experience. Travel with us, take the jobs only as a trainer or an adviser. What I'm offering can solve problems for both of us. We need numbers and experience, and I sense you could use some help with this one," he said, motioning to Cendra.

Cendra glowered. Everyone was treating her as hardly a person, something she had expected once she was labeled a Scarbearer. What angered her more than others treating her this way was that it only served to confirm the reality she had struggled to deny.

"I mean no disrespect," Brandt explained to Cendra. "I sense a fiery spirit in you, one that matches your talents." His eyes fell to her glowing hands. "I only mean that with someone new to this life, it can be very hard to adjust. I think you need a pack; more people to help you with this transition."

Cendra considered his words for a few moments. She could linger with Fionna outside the walls of the Port of Shayenir setting twigs on fire, but with no purpose or direction, it held no appeal. Her hands cooled and she looked toward Fionna, who nodded a silent agreement.

"Let's talk over the details," Fionna acquiesced, "Dinner tonight, on me. Your little Quiet looks like it could use a good meal."

"You are in quite the hurry, aren't you?" Raure followed closely behind Brandt and Tannah as they weaved through passersby on the busy street.

"We can't be late to this meeting. Too much rests on its outcome," Brandt replied, deftly sidestepping a slow-moving couple and squeezing by an oncoming man as he stepped in front of them.

"Are you sure this is a good idea? That girl—Cendra, was it? She's trouble, I can feel it. Did you see her eyes when you were saying she must be a handful? If looks could kill, you'd be someone's coat by now." Tannah was gracefully trailing Brandt. She moved with ease, navigating the crowd as if they weren't even there.

Brandt stopped suddenly and turned to look back at Tannah and Raure.

"We have no choice. We need experience and numbers to get jobs, they give us both, on paper at least. If you have another idea—*any* other idea—I'm all ears."

"Nope. Just don't like her."

"You're going to have to give her a chance. We need work." Brandt quickly pivoted to resume heel-and-toeing, but ran smack into a uniformed soldier leading a group of ten in the opposite direction.

"Well, by Armine's golden tits! If it isn't the illustrious Captain Brandt!" The man pointed to the ground and whistled. "Down, boy." He turned back to his comrades, laughing. "This was our last captain— my captain—until we were attacked by a pack of barghests. *Forty* men, all dead. All save myself, and this ... thing."

A low rumble began in the deepest part of Brandt's throat as his claws and teeth began to lengthen. Raure placed a calming hand on Brandt's shoulder.

"A shame that, of those survivors, the only one to witness your heroics during that fight was shunned as a Scarbearer, don't you think, Captain Haver?" Brandt growled.

The captain flushed red, "Fortunate, indeed, that the inquiry panel knew better than to trust the word of a tainted beast."

Brandt made to lunge with Raure and Tannah struggling to hold him back.

"Put your dog on a leash before I have my men put him down."

"They can try," Tannah raised her hands displaying crackling purple orbs of light, and smiled.

Nearly taking the bait, Captain Haver paused when he remembered where they were. Stone Row was no place to start a fight with Scarbearers. The area was teaming with them, and they had no love for him. Some had even stopped what they were doing to watch the exchange. Likely, they were waiting for an excuse to jump in.

"They aren't worth the trouble. Carry on." Captain Haver led his group around them and down the street, eyeing Brandt the whole way.

Brandt's claws receded as he watched the group walk away; the rumble remained, though quiet.

"What was that all about?" Tannah asked as she turned back toward Brandt.

Raure left no time for a response, "Well, you are quite popular, aren't you? I hope we meet no other old friends. We haven't the time to catch up."

He stepped to the side and made a sweeping gesture, offering the path forward to Brandt. Brandt paused briefly, glowering in the direction of his former comrades before continuing on, nodding his silent appreciation to Raure.

"Are you ready to order?" The waitress glanced back and forth between Fionna and Cendra.

"We are actually waiting on some friends. Could we just get some water for now?" Fionna replied.

"Certainly. I will be right back."

Cendra stopped her.

"Before you go, where did the name 'The Dinner Hell' come from?"

The smile vanished from the waitress's face, she glanced at Fionna, whose face had turned beet red, then, straightening her back, turned back to Cendra.

"It's 'The Dinner *Bell*', actually. The letter 'B' on the sign has just faded in an unfortunate manner. The owner will be fixing the sign soon." She quickly turned and hurried away.

"It's a nickname!" Fionna laughed, "Once that 'B' started to fade, everyone took up that name as it fit well with the atmosphere and food. No one ever calls it that to the staff and owners!"

"Why didn't you warn me?"

"I didn't think I had to. Who would ever name a restaurant 'The Dinner Hell'? It should have been obvious."

It was now Cendra's face that had flushed red.

"It's fine," Fionna smiled, "I don't think she will be back for a while, though. Maybe we should discuss this offer from Brandt. What do you think about it?"

"I don't know, exactly. I wouldn't say I'm excited about it. Everything has been coming at me so quickly. Part of me wants it all to stop, I've had enough change in the last several weeks to last a lifetime. At the same time, in comparison to everything else that has happened, this seems to be a pretty minor change, so why not?"

"I think it may be necessary for your development. I'm not excited about it myself, I'm afraid it's our best option. We would have some help developing your skills. I think we need all the help we can get."

"What's keeping them? I'm starving!" Cendra's stomach groaned audibly as she used her fork to draw invisible pictures on the table cloth that could only charitably be described as white.

"Patience, Cendra. If there is one trait you need to master above all others, it's patience. Patience with yourself, and with others. They will be here in due time, certainly before we are done in by hunger." Fionna had made sure not to let this teachable moment slip by. "Porter would have been completely justified if he had kicked us out of his office after your rude behavior today. Lucky for us, he showed you patience, patience you did not show to him, and was willing to go to work on our request." She paused to let it sink in. "As far as our expected guests, I would not worry. Brandt seemed to have a military air about him. If he is late, he will have a good reason. I am sure they will. ... Ah! You see? Here they are now."

"About time!" Cendra rose, following Fionna, who had done so to greet their guests.

"Apologies. We were met by an unwelcoming welcome party. The delay was unavoidable." Raure reached to shake their hands.

"No trouble, I hope." Fionna's concern was obvious on her face as her eyes scanned the entryway behind them.

"Nothing we couldn't handle," Tannah boasted, donning her toughest posture.

Brandt sat down immediately, avoiding any pleasantries. "Perhaps we should get down to business."

Fionna stared at him for a moment before looking back to the others. "Is he always like this?"

"Rude? Yes." Tannah answered with a smirk.

"Not usually to this degree, however. I fear his mood has been soured by Captain ... Haver, was it?" Raure looked to Brandt, but only got a grunt in response.

"Oh, Haver! Of course!" Fionna took a seat next to Brandt, patting him on the hand. "He's just a little prick that has let his station go to his head. It's best to just ignore him, dear."

"I got the impression that they have a history, it seems as if they despise each other." Tannah offered.

"Who could hate that face?" Cendra asked, smirking behind her water glass.

Tannah's eyes darted from Cendra to Brandt, fearing some sort of angry response. His brow furrowed momentarily before softening as he let out a small chuckle. She sighed before joining in the laugh. Soon the whole table was laughing.

As the laughter faded, Brandt leaned forward, "Have the two of you considered our deal?"

"We have," Fionna nodded, "but we need to know exactly who we are dealing with. I'd like to have dinner and talk first. Let's save business for the end of the night."

Brandt exhaled sharply. "What do you want to know?"

"What we are eating, for starters." Fionna peered down at her menu, ignoring Brandt's impatience.

Cendra slapped the table. "Thank the goddesses!"

As the meals came to the table, Cendra picked up her cutlery. She was ready to dive in, when she caught sight of Raure. His eyes were closed and he was almost inaudibly chanting. She did not recognize any of the specifics, as he practiced a religion that was utterly foreign to her, but she could see he was giving thanks for a meal. It was something she knew well, but had let herself forget since her exile. Her face flushed at the thought of her mother's disappointment as she bowed her head in prayer. As she finished, her eyes lifted just in time to catch

Fionna's pleased gaze moving from her back over to Raure.

"If I'm not mistaken, that was a prayer to Gairina. Yochi is a lovely religion. You don't often see it practiced outside of the Drywilds." Fionna offered a kind smile to let Raure know her curiosity was friendly.

"One does not leave paradise by choice. Those who have were forced, as I was. Most find themselves lost not only physically, but spiritually. It is no surprise that Yochi is a rare sight." He smiled at Cendra. "I found it difficult to stay connected with Gairina myself."

"I am not sure I care to continue following the Triune. I was the one who was abandoned." Cendra stabbed at a cube of meat on her dish.

"I certainly understand that. I would offer that it was the people that abandoned you, not your faith, but I will press you no more on it."

As Raure turned his attention to his meal, an awkward silence fell over the table. Tannah watched as they all fidgeted with their food.

"I want to hear about Haver!" She blurted out, trying to avoid the silence.

"I have to say I am interested, as well." Fionna brought a loaded fork to her mouth as she stared at Brandt.

Brandt pushed his plate away. Staring at the table, he sighed.

"Haver and I served together. He was an officer cadet back then. His father was a colonel, which is how he got an officer rank at all. He was green and not overly bright. Our colonel had put me in charge of a troop and sent us on routine patrol south of this very city. He left the choice of men to me, save for Haver. Haver was to get as much non-combat experience as we could give him—something the colonel had requested, trying to make an officer out of his son, who as far as we could tell was indifferent at best.

"My second lieutenant was an easy choice, Parsons. I grew up with him, we enlisted together and moved up the ranks together. I trusted him with my life, and he thought he could trust me with his." Brandt took in a slow shaky breath and let it out slowly. "As we neared the end of our patrol, someone cried out 'Barghest!'"

Fionna gasped and dropped her fork.

"It's you! The scarred survivor! I remember that attack. It was all anyone could talk about. A pack of barghests that close to the city was unheard of."

"What happened?" Tannah couldn't believe what she was hearing; Brandt was famous.

"They were on us in a flash. Barghests are fast, quiet, and vicious. Honestly, it was amazing we had any warning at all. That soldier saved the lives of Haver, Parsons, and myself by catching sight of them when he did."

"I only know of two survivors, though." Fionna shook her head, not understanding what she heard.

"Parsons had somehow fought off two barghests, I had killed one. There were twelve barghests, five were dead, the remaining seven were still attacking the surviving men, who I estimated to be about eleven, not counting we three officers. I gave the order to retreat toward the woods, where we could disperse. Our only hope was to spread out. It worked, I suppose, but only for the three of us. We had stuck together, thinking as a bigger group we could draw at least a few of them away from the other men. We were ignored. The sounds we heard as they found each man ..." His voice faltered. "It was so hard to listen to, knowing we couldn't do anything, and were very likely next. Haver was beginning to panic. Though I knew it was coming, I wasn't ready for how quickly it happened. He was off like a bolt. I reached for him, but he was beyond my grasp.

"Running around, causing a commotion like that, we knew he wasn't long for this world, and it looked as though we were right. One of the dogs was bearing down within seconds. I leapt to my feet, but Parsons was quicker. He met the barghest just before it reached Haver, and laid open a terrible gash along its ribs. It spun immediately to meet him, sinking its teeth into the forearm he had raised to shield his throat. By the time I had gotten to them, the barghest was thrashing him around like a doll. I sank my blade into the beast. It dropped my friend and turned on me, but it was weak. Knowing its strength was failing, the beast became rushed and wild in its attacks. After the first few, I was able to dodge its lunges fairly easily. I waited for my opening one faltered jump, and I had it. I buried my blade into its brain through the left eye.

"I spun around, expecting another dog, and found nothing. Then my eyes fell on Parsons. Just laying there..." His voice cracked again. Brandt fell silent and stared down at his drink.

"I'm so sorry." Tannah placed her hand on Brandt's. "I didn't know."

Fionna let a moment pass before filling in the blanks of the story.

"So, you and Haver were the only survivors. Given your present affliction, I can only assume you picked up your Scar during this fight. The army needed someone to blame, that was an easy choice for them, since Haver's dad was a colonel, and you were now a Scarbearer."

"More or less, I was destined for the blame anyway, as the commanding officer. What gets my hackles up, is that Haver's account painted himself as a hero, trying to save Parsons, only failing because I got in the way."

"Thank you for sharing that. I know it couldn't have been easy. For what it's worth, I believe you." Fionna looked around the table as the others nodded in agreement. "We all do, and so I have made my decision. Cendra and I will join your Quiet. When do you want to start?"

Brandt's scowl faded and the hint of a smile took its place.

"As soon as tomorrow, if we can. I definitely got the impression from Porter that there was plenty of work. I will go at dawn to discuss it with him."

"Getting right after it. Okay, but we don't rush into anything. I will insist on a good plan for every Quieting," Fionna pointed her fork at Brandt to drive her point.

"Of course, I'd have it no other way." Brandt's shoulders relaxed, and he shot a smile at Raure and Tannah as he lifted a forkful of food to his mouth.

CHAPTER 8
THE METHOD IN THE MARCH

"Have any of you been to Bellerenth?" Fionna asked, poking at the embers of the fire with a forked branch she had been using to cook a jinsuan sausage. They had traveled all day after Brandt had convinced Porter to recommend their new Quiet for a small job in Bellerenth to eradicate a hellcat that had been stalking the village.

The group collectively answered in the negative.

"I have," she continued. "Our kind is not popular there."

"We're not popular anywhere," Tannah replied, rolling her eyes at the absurdity of the warning.

"True enough. What I mean is that Bellerenth is full of hushes."

"Hushes?" Cendra had never heard the term.

"Hushes ..." Fionna repeated. She then paused for a second, realizing why Cendra would not know the word. " ... People who are fearful of magic, like the ones who shunned you. We should stick together. No one ventures off alone. We go in together, do the job fast, collect the money and get out. We need to be very respectful to everyone. ...” She turned her eyes to Cendra. “ ... especially the ones who don't deserve it.” Fionna looked around the group to be sure they all understood. Seeing that they were all in agreement, she continued. “This sounds like a small job. I'm leaving it to the three of you. Cendra is going to watch with me until she can get more control. I will be right here if it turns out to be more than we expected.”

Cendra hung her head. She knew that Fionna was right, but she felt like an outcast among outcasts.

Brandt stood up from his seat by the fire. He had been considering this hunt since they left the Port of Shayenir. He turned toward Raure and Tannah, who had turned back to their target practice. Tannah had been lobbing sparks at rocks and sticks that Raure tossed up for her. Her aim was improving steadily, snapping them sometimes before they left his hand, causing him to jerk his hand back and shake the shock out of his fingertips while glaring playfully at her. Brandt snapped his fingers at them, getting their attention.

“Listen, both of you. A hellcat is a deadly vicious animal. I should be able to hold my own with one for a short amount of time. No one else should enter within melee range of it until a decisive blow can be struck. Tannah, I'll need you to try and contain the cat to as small an area as you can with your lightning. You will need to be very careful—a hellcat is wild and can reverse direction unpredictably. Be fast and decisive, but don't hit any of us."

Tannah nodded nervously. "I can do it."

Raure put a hand on her shoulder.

"Your skills have improved greatly, little arcling. You will do quite well. I know it."

"Raure," Brandt continued, "You'll need to hang back. Stay just out of reach. I will be constantly trying to draw the cat's attention. If I can keep it on me, you should have ample opportunity to jump in and get your hand on it. Do not linger. Get in, lay hands on it, then get out."

Raure looked down at his hands, giving a long, slow exhale as his shoulders sagged.

"I know, friend," Brandt reassured. "It is my hope that it will just take but one touch for us to gain the upper hand. Weaken the beast enough to run it off."

Raure nodded.

"You aren't planning to kill it?" Fionna was intrigued.

"If necessary. It's easier to drive it away if we can manage it. Besides, if we can bring the clients the relief they need, it makes no difference in the end.

"Fair enough."

Brandt took in a deep breath and blew out a lengthy sigh. Tension sloughed off of his shoulders and he sat down with the slightest hint of a smile on his lips. He looked over the group. Cendra and Fionna were chatting quietly. Tannah and Raure had gone back to their target practice game. They were still two separate groups, and he was still unsure how they would all get along. He felt, though, for the first time, that he could make a Quiet out of them. This might actually work.

Cendra woke to the sound of Raure and Fionna talking over a pot of fire-brewed tea. She sat up and took in the scene. Dawn had just broken. Thick fog had set in overnight, and not much was visible beyond camp. Tannah was still asleep, and Brandt was missing. Shivering in the chill of the morning, she joined Fionna and Raure by the fire.

Raure greeted her with a smile and a warm cup of tea.

"Good morning, Cendra. I trust you slept well."

Cendra responded with a groan, lifting the cup toward him in a sincere, but labored expression of gratitude. She then sat quietly by the fire, sipping her tea, trying to get warm as she woke up. Sleeping outside was not yet something she had grown accustomed to.

Raure smiled knowingly at Fionna.

"You were saying that you were a ... Collector, was it?"

"Yes, with Cendra's parents actually." Fionna watched Cendra as she turned her ear to the conversation. "Collecting anything we could relating to magic. So much has been erased from history since the War of Silence."

"War of Silence?" Raure had not heard of any war by that name.

"We've recovered ancient texts that mention it. That's how they refer to it, but even in the texts it is an event in the distant past, and little is known about it. However, based on what has been found it seems that before the war, magic was tolerated—accepted, even. Immediately after, magic seemed to be purged from history."

Cendra had perked up; she had not expected to hear about her parents.

"My parents did this with you?"

"They were very rare indeed. Humans with no Scars who were interested in magic and actively working to restore ancient knowledge of it. They knew that ignorance and fear are joined at the hip; remove ignorance, and fear will follow. Oh look! Here comes breakfast."

Brandt had returned with some wild onions, berries, and a fat bird he had already cleaned and dressed—a hogfowl, large and fatty. Brandt made a spit out of some found sticks and hung the bird over the fire. Before long, it was dripping sizzling juices into the flames. Raure produced a pan from his bag and placed it below the spit to catch the fat and juices before he cut up the onions and added them and the berries to the pan. Reaching again into his bag, he pulled out a pouch that contained a variety of bundled herbs he had grown in his garden. He chose a few and added them to the pan.

Tannah was roused by the smell of a delicious meal. She slept heavily, as the young often do, but she differed from Cendra in that she woke up with what seemed to be her ever-present cheeriness. She stretched out one final yawn and came bounding to the fire to enjoy breakfast.

"Are we leaving straight away?" she asked as she dug into breakfast, seemingly starving.

"Yeah." Brandt replied as he watched her eat. After nearly a month of spending every day with her, he was still astonished at her appetite. She must have eaten her weight in food each week.

"We are nearly halfway there, I gather, " Fionna offered. "I suppose we will travel all day today, and get one more night in before arriving early tomorrow?" The statement was more of a question.

"I think we could be there tonight," Brandt replied.

"I don't see the need to rush. If we get there tonight it would be just to sleep. We would not be able to actually do anything until tomorrow. Why not take our time, and show up in the morning, well rested?"

"I don't see the point in lagging. Let's get there and get the job done." Brandt could see her logic, but he was anxious to get to the task at hand. It had been a long wait, and a quick success would give his team confidence. Besides, the more time they spent idle was more time to worry—and of worry, he had had his fill.

Fionna could see that, right or wrong, Brandt was not going to be swayed. "Alright, No sense in sitting about, then."

She got to her feet and began breaking camp. Brandt and Raure quickly jumped up to help. Tannah got to her feet, still trying to finish her meal. Cendra's head dropped. She just wanted to sit by the fire for a few more moments. She stood with a sigh, not wishing the others to see her sitting around as they worked.

The fog lifted by midday, though it had foretold the atmosphere of the afternoon. The sky was gray and thick. As is often the case, the weather had forced its mood on the people living with it. The Quiet had been walking along the northern bank of the Korubant in silence for what had seemed to be an eternity.

Cendra watched as Tannah and Raure worked on the mage's skills. Raure would throw his dagger into stumps or logs along the way, Tannah would try to hit it in flight with electric bolts. Cendra had noted her steady improvement even in the short time they had traveled together. She found herself envious of Tannah's control.

"Careful now, little arc! I'm not keen to know the pain of those bolts," Raure said, smiling at Tannah.

Fionna had noticed Cendra watching them.

"Some practice would do you good, as well."

"Do you think that's a good idea, so close to everyone?"

"I'm sure it would be fine, but for the sake of safety let's hang back a little bit to give ourselves some space."

As the others carried on, Fionna took Cendra's right hand and positioned its palm up in front of her.

"I want you to try to create a flame and hold it in your hand."

"You mean without wood or anything?"

"Yes. I don't think you need it. Give it a try."

Cendra focused on her open palm. Within seconds, her hand was on fire, her fingers and palm wreathed in a soft flame.

"Amazing! Does that not hurt?"

"I don't feel anything."

"Well it's not quite what I meant, but it could be a handy trick. Put it out and do it again."

The flame disappeared and reappeared as quickly as Fionna had asked. Cendra could not hide her excitement. She lit her hands back and forth over and over again. Fionna watched, letting her have her moment of fun.

"Alright—now that you seem to have that down, try it like I asked. Try to make a suspended flame above your palm."

Cendra tried for several minutes, but this proved to be beyond her grasp—she could not conjure the flame as asked. Fionna chose a stick from the ground and put the tip of it above Cendra's palm.

"Can you light the tip of the stick?" Fionna asked.

Cendra immediately produced flame, burning the end of the stick. Fionna took the stick away and tried to get Cendra to repeat it without a prop to burn, again to no avail.

"Well, let's not fall too far behind. As we are walking, I want you to keep trying. Imagine something suspended above your hand. Visualize it. I think this is something you can do."

Cendra continued practicing for hours of walking, never quite getting it. She thought she'd see smoke or a small wisp of flame appear, but any that did were gone as quickly as they appeared. To keep her spirits up, she would light up her hands and wave them around, admiring her newly dis-covered talent.

"Wow! That's some trick," Tannah exclaimed, nudging Raure to have a look at Cendra's hand.

"That is quite impressive, Cendra! You are in-deed coming along, are you not?" Raure said, nodding his congratulations to Fionna as well.

"We're going to need it," Brandt said, sniffing the air. "The rain is coming in fast and hard. Likely a pretty bad storm."

"We had better find some shelter," Fionna said.

"We don't have time for shelter. By the time we find it, we'll already be soaked. We should press on. A few more hours and we will be there," Brandt argued.

"Perhaps, that is if we can make good time in a storm—a big if. When we get there we will be soaked and worn out, possibly sick. We should find a dry place dry and warm by a fire, until the storm passes at least," Fionna was insistent.

Brandt quietly growled to himself as he weighed Fionna's words.

"We'll stick to the edge of the river so we don't get lost. The Korubant is our path to Bellerenth. Along the way, there may be some dry overhangs carved out of the cliffs. We stop only if we find a good spot."

They arrived at Bellerenth hours later than planned, exhausted and water logged. The only overhangs that the cliffs offered had been swallowed by the rising water of the Korubant. They dragged themselves through town to a small inn called the Goose and Down.

Entering through the front door, they found the taproom fairly quiet. Not a surprise, given the hour. Tannah and Cendra headed straight for the hearth, while Raure and Fionna found a seat. Brandt approached the steward behind the bar.

"Two rooms. Is the kitchen still serving?"

"It's late." The innkeeper spoke with a low tone under a lower brow, visibly leery of Brandt's imposing presence. "The kitchen is closed, but we still have some stew. I'll hang the pot on the fire. Rooms are an Armine a piece. Meals are included."

Brandt reached into his pouch and began to count out coins. One Ilona and some cops. He sighed and looked back toward the group, and saw Fionna already on her way over with gold in her hand.

"Two Armines?" She handed them to the steward. "Could we get that stew out here right away, Goren? We are starving. I do not suppose you have got any of that bread Nefil makes, have you?"

"Fionna!" He darted his eyes around the room, and pulling her aside, he addressed her quietly. "I'm sorry I didn't recognize you, but it has been ages. What are you after now? By the look of your company, something a little more dangerous than the—what was it—compass?"

"You know very well it was a sextant, and you still owe me for that little mishap. Anyway it's nothing like that. This is a Quiet I have just joined," she paused. "Stop looking around like that! You are making me nervous. I made sure no one was around before we came in."

"Interesting! Well, it is good to see you. I'll go get that food. We might have some butter cakes, as well," Goren offered, leaving for the kitchen.

"You might have said something," Brandt muttered.

"Talking to you seems like wasted breath."

Brandt smirked, "Talking to anyone is wasted breath."

They rejoined Raure at his table. Brandt dropped into his chair like a tossed bag of stones. Fionna was not much more graceful. They sat in wearied silence, watching as the young ones warmed their bones.

"I suppose you're here for the hellcat, then?" Goren said, as he laid bread on the table.

The bread had no more than touched the table before Fionna broke off a chunk and bitten into it. With her mouth still full, she answered in the affirmative.

Goren moved to the hearth with the pot of stew, "It is a beast, truly. That is all anyone is talking about here." He squeezed by the girls and hung the pot in the hearth. "It's as big as a four-horse wagon. I hope you know what you are in for."

"We can handle ourselves," Cendra snapped.

"No disrespect, Miss. It is just that the thought of having to face that thing chills me through. Only thinking of your safety."

"Thank you for your concern, Goren. Please disregard her impertinence. She is tired and hungry, and hasn't yet learned to hold her tongue," Fionna offered, giving Cendra a scolding look from under her brow.

"Not to worry. I was young myself once. The stew will be warm soon. I will fetch some cider and butter cakes." He was off as quickly as he had appeared.

Cendra rolled her eyes and turned back toward the fire. Tannah, having seen the contempt on Cendra's face, let out a snorting laugh and leaned her shoulder into Cendra with a playful nudge. Cendra tried to fight it, but found herself laughing along with her.

"They are hitting it off," Fionna motioned toward the girls giggling by the fire. "Thought for sure Tannah had daggers out for Cendra."

"They have youth in common. They are linked in a way we cannot match." Raure leaned back in his seat, draping his right arm over the back with an easy grace that projected his relaxed mood. He spun a silver Ilona through the pallid gray fingers of his left hand on the table.

Raure's posture was contrasted sharply by that of Brandt. He sat on the front edge of his seat hunched over with his forearms on his knees. "Is Tannah prepared?"

Raure smirked. "Are any of us?" Seeing that Brandt was not amused, he continued. "She knows that plan, she is remarkably sharp for her age, and has been practicing nearly every waking moment. She has never done anything like this though. We need to be able to handle this without her if it comes to it."

"I can keep him distracted long enough for you to get in there. ..." Brandt's already serious expression became heavy. "You may have to take it farther than you like."

"I am prepared to do what is needed. You will have my support, friend."

Brandt's expression relaxed. "I'm off to bed, then."

"What of the stew?" Fionna asked.

"Stomach's not in the mood. In the morning we are to meet Mayor Frenell right here. I will see you all then."

CHAPTER 9

THE FIRE IN THE FIELD

Cendra walked into the great room to find the mayor already in conversation with Brandt and Fionna. He was a short, round man with a thin mustache and large eyes that appeared too close together on his face. His mannerisms were wild as he talked, matching the level of his voice. She could hear the conversation clearly even from a distance.

" ... fight fire with fire—er, that is to say ... I mean to say that this thing cannot be stopped by any righteous means, so we must resort to your kind. Lesser of two evils, I suppose."

Cendra's face began to flush. Her mind flamed at his words, first with embarrassment, then shame. Here she was, part of the "unrighteous, lesser of two evils." It grated at her soul to know this was how she would be perceived. She felt the shame of being a Scarbearer, and then shame for being ashamed of it. Both broke under the weight of her rage—rage at the mayor for thinking this way, then rage for herself for knowing she still felt the same way.

Mayor Frenell's face grew pale as his eyes fixed on Cendra stalking toward him over Brandt's shoulder.

"Keep that demon back! I won't have your cursed magic used in city limits!" While his voice carried the force of power and authority, his steps carried nothing but fear as he stumbled backward.

Brandt and Fionna turned as Raure and Tannah intercepted Cendra. They spoke to her calmly, but with urgency.

"Cendra, stop. This will accomplish nothing."

Cendra sneered at the pair of them. "What the hell are you on about? Get out of my way."

"Cendra, look at yourself ..." Tannah said, gesturing downward.

Dancing flames engulfed Cendra's arms from her clenched fists to her elbows, tiny embers wafting from the lashing tongues of the flames. Her footfalls seared the floorboards, faint wisps of smoke drifting upward in her fiery wake. She stopped, silent, the realization setting in. The flames died away, and Cendra stormed out into the street.

Tannah stepped forward, hoping to ease the tension.

"Hey, everything's alright, no damage done." Tannah looked back as Goren doused the smoldering tracks with water from a mop bucket. "Well ... Not much damage, anyway."

Raure nudged Tannah out of the way and stepped between her and the mayor.

"No one was hurt, everyone here is safe. I realize how it looked, but she didn't mean harm; we aren't monsters."

"Monsters are exactly what your kind are. This contract was a mistake—here we are, trading a single monster for five others!"

The words had no more than left the mayor's mouth when Brandt snatched his shirt collar and pulled the diminutive man nose to nose with himself. His brow furrowed, his fangs bared. He growled deep, so deep that Frenell felt it rattle through his ribs.

Frenell flinched, hiding his face behind his hands. "I'm sorry! I—"

"My patience with you has reached its end, so listen well. We will remove your monster, we will collect our pay, and then we will depart before the piss has dried from your trousers. Once our business is concluded, you will be safe, never having to lay eyes on us again—so long as you *mind your fucking mouth.*"

The mayor was out of the door in a flash. Brandt and Raure emerged from the door behind him to find Cendra sitting on the steps, chucking pebbles into the street.

She did not look as Raure slowly sank down to sit on the step next to her. He gently rested a hand on her shoulder.

"Cendra, are you alright?"

"Alright?" She scoffed. "You heard that self-righteous prick. He's right; I'm a monster."

"You have it wrong, Cendra. You are no monster. You have a Scar—but that means nothing. We all do. You simply have not had the time it takes to learn to control it."

Brandt pointed across the street to Frenell, running frantically down the street to the Counting House.

"You're certainly no more a monster than that sad little man." He leaned low to her ear. "I think he shit himself."

Cendra desperately tried to fight the hint of a short laugh, but failed.

"That's better. Now get off your ass; we have work."

Cendra rose to her feet with a sigh and stepped in the direction of the inn before stopping.

"... Thank you. Even if I don't believe it, I think I needed to hear it."

Tannah emerged from the town hall and stepped next to Brandt. They watched Cendra walk away silently for a few moments before Tannah spoke up.

"Are we sure this is a good decision?"

Brandt continued staring wordlessly.

"That wasn't just a problem, it could have been a catastrophe. It's not even that she almost cost us our first hunt; she could have burned this place and all the people in it to the ground."

Raure chuckled. "Yes, that was quite the spectacle, but Cendra is very new to this life. Cendra is understandably quite upset; you must try to understand—"

"Understand what? She was out of control!"

"... You must understand the fundamental difference between you and Cendra. Between you and *us*. Once you have learned to control your talents, you could simply one day decide to stop. There's nothing to stop you simply ceasing to conjure your sparks. You could return to your home and lead a perfectly normal life and so long as you chose none would ever know the magic inside you. Now look at Brandt."

She looked up at him to find Brandt's gaze already on her—his ears high, his fur swaying in the breeze—and a sadness in his eyes as he listened.

"The places we once called home can never be again. We cannot hide what we are; not in any way that would survive scrutiny. Your gift is hidden away until you call on it. Cendra's is branded upon her face. She is alone and she is scared. For all that she has now been robbed of, we understand why she is angry, for it was taken from us, as well."

Tannah stared silently at Brandt. In all their time traveling together, she had seen the consequence of bearing the Scar firsthand, but had never stopped to truly understand his reality. To be a Scarbearer was not some mere occasional inconvenience—it was to be branded a pariah forevermore.

Her eyes welled. She lunged forward, wrapping her arms around Brandt as tightly as she could muster. He shot Raure a stunned look before taking her shoulders gently in his hands.

"Hey, no. ... It's alright, there's no need for that. You recognized a danger and you were right to speak your mind about it."

She looked up to see him smiling down.

"I am proud of you."

"You're only half right, Raure." She turned to him as she wiped tears from her cheeks. "Magic is part of me. It's always there, whether you see it or not—I will never forsake it. Why should you have to hide? Why should *we* ... ?"

"I did not mean to suggest—" She had caught him by surprise. "I apologize. You are right, we should not—but life often is not fair. We must play the cards we are dealt, and sometimes the dealer is dirty. That is too large a battle for us alone, and the little battles demand our attention at present."

Brandt chimed in. "The battle of food and shelter. For that we need coin, and for coin we need Cendra." He leaned down to meet Tannah at eye level. "Please, just give her a chance. Besides, yesterday I saw the pair of you thick as thieves. Nothing has changed; if this works out, it works out. If not, we will figure it out." He tousled her hair with a chuckle. "And between the two of you, so far I have only seen one of you actually set something on fire."

"Har har, Scruffy—and that was an *accident*, by the way."

"Well, in all fairness it is not as if Cendra was trying to set the place ablaze." Raure stood with a deep stretch; his folded hands arching skyward. "Power like we have—power like she has—is a grave danger if allowed to run wild. She would benefit from experienced support; not just for her sake ... " They watched as she disappeared down the street.

"... but for the sake of those around her."

The smell of embers danced on Brandt's nose as they marched out into the fields surrounding Bellerenth. Two entire barley fields lay empty and blackened, no doubt burned by the cat's fire. This would not be the first hellcat Brandt had faced; in his brief time with another group, he had been forced to contend with one of these beasts and it had nearly cost him his life. He remembered the scent vividly. Where others might only smell fire, he smelled hot coal and burning fur—a mane of rage and fury. He crouched close to the ground and examined the air as his nose drew him toward an imprint on the ground—a large paw print, twice the size of Brandt's own boot sole, the mud around it dried, scorched, and cracked. More could be seen in the growth along the trail, leading toward the fields where smoke still rose into the sky.

"Figures. For a hellcat, farmland would make both a home and easy hunting grounds." He cast his eye into the distance where the greenery was pockmarked with sears and burn lines. "The fields here form a sort of pinwheel with the sheds and pens in the center; presumably there is—or was— livestock on the far side. Raure, keep Tannah close to you and circle around to the right, I will go around the left. If you encounter it first, protect Tannah and I will come to engage. Tannah, keep clear and, if it finds you, your first priority is to get away. Your immediate second priority is contain- ment. Clear?"

She shifted the bandolier on her chest that held a number of iron darts and clutched her javelin close. "Okay. I will do my best."

Raure laid a gloved hand on her shoulder. "You can do this." He gave her a warm smile. "I will en- sure your safety."

Brandt gave each of them a nod, and they set out leaving Cendra and Fionna to observe.

Tannah followed on Raure's heels as they circled the ashen remains of the barley fields, her spear quivering in her hands. She watched as Brandt circled the other direction until she lost sight of him completely behind the fields and fences.

"I—I'm scared."

Raure turned to her and knelt down, scanning around to ensure they were safe. He smiled into her eyes.

"Young one, as long as we are careful and follow the advice we were given, Brandt will be safe, and so will you." He tousled her hair. "I've seen what you can do and I have confidence in you. Simply do the best you can, and we will handle the rest." His face suddenly became more somber. "However, take care how close you follow—when my gloves are removed, it is imperative that you do not touch my hands."

Tannah nodded nervously.

They proceeded onward cautiously. The smell of burned grass and wood hung heavy in the air, but heavier still was the silence. The only sound was the breeze on the fields, interspersed with the occasional crackle from the fire or creaking wood. Upon reaching the west end of the fields, Raure stopped. His eyes narrowed to a squint as he studied the fields. Brandt had surmised correctly that there had been livestock in the far fields; he saw terrorized sheep huddled together in the far corner of the field, dismembered and burned corpses between them and their pen. In the center of the fields facing outward were livestock pens and barns and a couple of tool sheds. Looking back the way they came, he could see Fionna and Cendra in the distance. All else was still—Brandt had not come around the other side, and, as yet, there was no sign of the hellcat.

"What do we do now?" Tannah gripped her javelin tight.

"We keep watch—if the beast attempts to flee this way, it will be on us to prevent its escape, lest we be forced to hunt it down anew. You might consider putting a dart in the ground here." Raure began unfastening the buckles on his gloves.

Tannah did as advised, and then they waited. Tension saturated the air as the minutes crept by, Tannah fidgeting nervously with her javelin.

A loud crash cut the silence as Brandt and the hellcat burst through the wall of the livestock pen, spilling out into the field. Brandt tumbled on the ground a distance before quickly righting himself on one knee. Fear and fury began transfiguring his body courtesy of his Scar. Coarse jet-black fur surged up from his skin as he quickly struggled to remove his jacket, his limbs and jaws elongating with a series of sickening crunches. The hellcat was up again in an instant and charged at him with a mighty roar, its blazing paws charring the earth as it ran. Brandt clutched his greatsword in one massive hand and rushed the animal in a bestial three-legged sprint. At the last moment, he fell into a leg-first slide, slipping under its snapping jaws, and shoved upward hard with his shoulder, pushing off the ground with his legs to send it airborne. The hellcat spun in the air before landing with a grace unexpected for its size about three meters away. The pair circled each other, snarling.

The two danced perilously. The hellcat would have pounced and disemboweled an ordinary person in an instant, but the additional height and mass afforded by his transformation made Brandt not-so-easy prey. As they circled, they traded occasional cautious swipes, probing each other for weaknesses.

Just beyond the fenceline, Brandt saw Cendra charging toward them, Fionna hot on her heels. He could see that Fionna was yelling something, but could not hear it over the crackle of fire and the hellcat's snarls. Cendra's eyes were aflame. She stopped short of the fenceline and, as she raised her hands skyward, a huge gout of fire burst from the earth under the beast.

Fionna caught up to Cendra and they watched as the flames subsided. They hellcat stood unharmed; its fur blazing even more mightily than before.

Brandt's fury spilled over.

"What the fuck are you trying to do, make it feel at home?!"

That was all the time the hellcat needed to strike. It swiped him in the chest with one enormous paw, the force sending him flying into what was left of the wall of the livestock pen they had just burst through. He slammed into the wall with a cough accompanied by a mist of blood.

With a thud, a dart sunk into the splintered wall of the livestock pen above his head. In his periphery, Brandt saw that Raure and Tannah had caught up to them, Raure keeping himself between the mage and the fight. The sound of the dart hitting the wall had briefly caught the attention of the great cat and, seizing the momentary diversion, Brandt sprung forward, a whirlwind of claw, tooth, and steel.

Brandt successfully laced the beast open in three places—great gashes across its front legs and chest—but not without cost. With a horrid yelp, the hellcat's fiery blood sprayed across Brandt's chest and face, searing away fur, scorching his skin, and burning his eyes. He recoiled, blinded. The hellcat did not waste a moment and with a blood-curdling roar it pounced, savagely beating Brandt as he tried helplessly to keep his sword between him and the beast.

An ear-splitting scream rang out as the hellcat's flames wavered; it roared furiously as the intense heat faded. Through blurry eyes, Brandt could see Raure at the beast's haunches, a blackened hand pressed against the once-blazing fur. Raure screamed in pain as his cursed palms channeled the living flame out of the hellcat's body and into his own arm, then fell to the ground, writhing in agony.

Tannah trembled, holding her pike in front of her. The hellcat stood over her companions menacingly. It may have been wounded and weakened, but it was still standing.

"Brandt!" she cried. "I don't know what to do!"

A small rock struck the beast in the temple. It turned to face Cendra, who was already clutching another fist-sized rock in her hand.

"Hey! Come and get me, you piece of shit!" It crept slowly toward her. Looking past the hellcat, she yelled to Tannah. "Containment, right?"

"I can't! Brandt is still holding his sword!"

Brandt struggled off the ground to his knees, blood spilling out of his mouth onto the ground before him.

"Just do it. You'll know when."

As quietly as he could manage, he brought himself to his feet, pain wracking his body. He lifted his sword, its weight becoming more cumbersome by the moment as darkness hung on the edges of his blurred sight. He steeled himself and watched as the hellcat stalked toward Cendra. Then, he lunged. Every step was agony before he leapt into the air, bringing the tip of his greatsword directly beneath him. The beast looked back too late—Brandt landed on its back and plunged the sword between two great ribs then fell to the ground, spent.

"Now!" Fionna yelled.

Tannah, her hands trembling and eyes watering, sent electricity coursing through her javelin. It arced wildly in great azure bolts between her and the greatsword lodged in the beast's chest cavity. The hellcat convulsed, shrieking and roaring for what felt an eternity, then fell to the ground—its great paws twitching intermittently as its fiery heart beat its last.

Tannah fell to her knees, her breath coming in ragged heaves. Her skin went cold as her terror caught up with her. Before her, the great beast lay dead, its flames extinguished. The field and pen were in flaming ruin. Brandt and Raure lay on the ground on either side of the hellcat's corpse, Raure clutching his arm in pain and Brandt burned and bleeding.

"Tannah," Raure managed through gritted teeth, "my satchel. Mortar and pestle, and the bottles labeled equflos, stopwort, and frosttooth. Quickly."

Her shaking hands sifted through the various bottles and tools in Raure's bag. She brought the requested items to him.

"What are you going to do?"

"Not me." He clenched his arm close to his chest. "You. I will tell you what to do. We need to stop Brandt's bleeding." He looked her directly in the eye. "All will be alright, but we must work quickly. In the mortar, grind one part equflos to two parts stopwort. Grind them to as fine a powder as you can, then add enough water to turn it into a paste. Apply the paste to all the open wounds you can find."

As quickly as she could manage, Tannah worked the mortar and pestle until she created a thick teal paste. She ran over to Brandt who lay face down, his blood making a black mud out of the charred soil. She attempted to roll him over, but his shifted shape had made him too heavy for her to lift.

"Help! Someone, please!"

The cry had no more than left her mouth before Fionna was there. She put her fingers gently under his shoulder and rolled him over with an ease that shocked Tannah. Three great jagged wounds crossed his chest, the skin and fur matted with blood. The left side of his face and neck had been seared horribly. She scooped a handful of the paste out of the mortar and began gently smearing it across the bleeding slashes. At nearly the instant the paste made contact with the wounds, she could hear it bubble and crackle as it turned a sour purple, and where it touched the bleeding seemed to cease instantly. Brandt's ragged breathing halted, and did not resume.

"Raure!" Tannah shrieked. "He's not breathing!"

He had struggled his way over to them.

"This is expected, it is an effect of stopwort. I will explain later. Take what remains of the paste, grind in one part frosttooth and add the mixture to my canteen then shake it vigorously."

Once more Tannah ground in the mortar until an icy green mush formed, then added it to the canteen. She shook as hard as she could for several seconds, and uncapped it. The smell was intense—floral and cold.

"What now?"

"Brandt needs to drink as much of that as he can. Due to the stopwort, you will need to force him to swallow. Pour in a mouthful then massage his throat to force it down. Save a third of the canteen."

Fionna pried Brandt's fanged jaws open and held them there. Tannah placed the canteen over his open maw and poured in a little of the pungent liquid. His one open eye drifted with an extreme laziness back and forth. She placed a palm on his throat and massaged downward, the liquid disappearing from his mouth, again and again until a little over half of the canteen had been drained. The heat she felt from the burns on his face began to fade, and she almost thought she saw them frost over in places.

"Fionna, please roll Brandt back over. His body's reactions are so slow right now that if he coughs face up, he will choke and die. Tannah, bring the canteen to me."

Fionna slowly rolled Brandt back to his stomach as Tannah sprinted the canteen over to Raure. His eyelids were low and heavy, his voice sinking by the moment, as if he were about to lose consciousness.

"Place the open canteen in front of me and step back."

Raure placed the open palm of his burned arm to the ground with a wince, and with his other hand picked up the canteen. He emptied its contents over his arm with an agonizing scream as the liquid crackled and popped, turning into a black sludge. Under his palm, a pale green glow filtered out between his hand and the earth as the burns on his arms faded and the charred black skin gave way to its original pallid gray. With a great sigh of relief, Raure fell back on his rear. "Excellent work, both of you. Thank you."

The three of them sat on the ground, exhausted, as Cendra looked on from several paces away. What was she doing here? All she had done since they arrived was make a bad situation worse, jeopardizing their lives by putting their prey in its element. The thought barely had time to make it across her mind when she heard the rattle of boards coming from the ruined livestock pen.

"You should all probably get back up if you can. ... The job might not be done." Cendra muttered with what confidence she had left. She looked at her companions, mostly spent. Only she and Fionna were still in any condition to defend themselves—and by this point she wondered what she could even contribute—but the hellcat was far faster than any of them. Running was not an option. If another one was here, it would be fight or die.

Fionna was on her feet and came to Cendra's side.

"Look at us, Fionna. We're all that's left."

"Aye. I'm sorry this happened to everyone. Perhaps I shouldn't have held us back—we are the only two here who can't be burned and my hesitation has cost them dearly."

Cendra's eyes fixed on the pen. She should have been terrified. For all she knew, she stood mere paces away from her end. She had seen the beast fell Brandt and Raure handily, and Brandt was an experienced fighter; until a mere few weeks ago she was just an ordinary person preparing for an ordinary life in an ordinary town. An ordinary person should run or hide. But no, she was not afraid. She was furious. Furious at Brandt for rushing the trip.

Furious at Fionna for telling her what to do. Furious at having all of this thrust upon her without any of her control. Furious for countless reasons, many of which she didn't even yet understand.

Enough. She strode forward so quickly Fionna had no time to protest. Cendra ripped Tannah's iron dart out of the wood and gripped the edge of what remained of the burned out wall of the livestock pen. She gripped so hard that flames burst from her knuckles and forearms and, with a great scream and pull, she ripped the remains of the wall free of the frame, sending it soaring over the fence. She braced her feet in the dirt, lowering herself closer to the ground in anticipation of the snarling beast that would be on her instantly—but it never came.

Her breath was hot in her nose as her eyes darted around the pen. There was nothing large enough in here for a hellcat of that size to hide under or behind. Another rattle of boards, and Cendra wheeled on her heels to face it. One more rattle, and Cendra saw the loose pile of debris that it came from. She sprang to it and with a roar she ripped the board away. Beneath, a ball of orange-red fur cowered.

Her fury faltered. She had braced herself to face death by claw or tooth, but not this. From the ball of fur peeked two cinder-brown eyes. No larger than one of her shoes, it shivered in the rubble—

the gentle blue flames in its fur faltering, a pathetic *mew* coming from it every few seconds.

Her rage drained from her, at least for the moment. She gazed at the little hellkitten. She thought of its parent lying lifeless on the ground a few meters away—a parent whose death she had been a participant in. It was too small to feed or defend itself; if left to its own devices it would die slowly from hunger. It would be a mercy to kill it now, quickly. In a closed fist, she raised the dart into the air.

She froze in place. The fist with the dart hung in the air as a thousand thoughts raced through her mind. This creature hadn't harmed anyone; it *couldn't* harm anyone as it was now. As an adult it could, yes, but even the great hellcat they had just killed wasn't acting out of malice. It had merely wanted to survive and to protect its young. The little eyes were locked on hers. Another desperate *mew*. The dart fell to her side.

She looked to her side to find that Fionna had been standing behind her.

"I—I can't."

A long pause.

"Because you are not a monster."

Fionna, Tannah, and Raure set camp there in the ruined field while Brandt lay motionless, face-down on the ground. Raure had instructed them not to move him; the stopwart had slowed all of his bodily functions while the frosttooth soothed his burns and the equflos healed his wounds. He would be incapacitated for the better part of a day, but for Brandt's slowed perception it would only seem a few minutes had passed. Indeed, the medicine had worked wonders already; he would have three new large scars across his chest, but the wounds had already closed and, aside from some missing fur, there was nearly no evidence left that he had been burned at all.

Cendra watched as they worked, the trembling hellkitten curled in her lap. Cendra had expected it to be hot to the touch. Though she suspected she was more or less impervious to heat now, she could still sense it. But the little kitten, small blue flames dancing in its fur, was little warmer than any other animal. It buried its face under her arm as it shook.

They sat in relative silence until dusk, each contemplating the now very real weight of their situation. The danger was no longer a potential—they had witnessed it firsthand. Their first job had nearly ended them.

"Is it always like this?" Tannah's voice still had a quiver to it. "If it is, I don't know if I can do this."

Raure remained silent, massaging his arm in its gauntlet wistfully.

"They're never the same, not really," Fionna said with a sigh. "Sometimes they are better. Sometimes it is far worse."

Cendra stroked the kitten in her lap.

"What we did today ... That hellcat may have eaten some sheep, but that's its nature isn't it? Wasn't it just out to survive? It hadn't hurt anyone and wasn't out to, at least not for any reason but to defend itself and live. What we did today—it felt like murder."

"There is a very real melancholy in it, yes." Raure locked eyes with her. "However, it was making its home in the fields these people use to feed their families. Look at the fields—its very presence made growing impossible, and if it had not been dealt with it would only have been a matter of time before it attacked someone working the fields, perceiving them to be encroaching on its territory. I do understand, though. It was beautiful, in its way, and we are what killed it."

"It was a job, and the job is done," groaned Brandt, who was now rolling onto his back. His form had begun shrinking back down to his usual size. "Can someone bring me the sewing kit from my bag? I have to stitch my godsdamned shirt back together again."

"Brandt!" Tannah grabbed his pack and ran to him. He winced as she hugged him tight.

"Thanks kid, but go easy on me—I'm still in a fair amount of pain." He removed the tattered shirt and rummaged through his pack, producing a small leather scroll case containing an assortment of needles and various threads and began meticulously stitching the torn shirt back together. This was clearly common practice for Brandt—looking closer at the shirt, Cendra noticed a great number of already existing stitches and patches.

Cendra looked down again to the kitten in her lap.

"This was a mistake. This one hunt nearly killed two of us because I don't know what I am doing, and for what? To help people who clearly hate us? I ..." The words ceased. She had a thousand more, but could not speak.

Brandt stopped stitching and laid his needle down. He looked around at his companions, exhausted and shaken.

"I am not a man of words. I haven't the tact for it. But don't think I don't feel the weight of what we've done here. I was a soldier. I have shed the blood of men I never knew for causes I did not understand, far more pointlessly than this." He looked into the campfire. "Maybe I'm a little desensitized, but I know some of you have never killed and I know that's a burden; a burden that never truly fades. Cendra, what I said to you during the fight was rash. I know you were only trying to help. I am not new to this life, but I know you are and I will try to remember that going forward. But while I am not a tactful man, I am a practical one. We are on a path that we cannot avoid—there are no other options available to us. All of you, look around. We are all marked by magic in a way that destroys any hope of fitting into a normal society. We're outcasts, whether we like it or not—we can't just go into town and pretend we'll fit in, they won't have us. Not all of us have Raure's gift for self sufficiency. Honestly, he'd probably be better off, but for the rest of us, it's either this or go live in squalor in Stone Row, judged by everyone around you and never knowing if you'll have the money for your next meal."

Raure let out a small chuckle, then walked to Brandt clapping a big leather mitt on his shoulder.

"Well, my friend—as motivational speeches go, that was ... lackluster, truth be told. But I left home for a reason. A multitude of them, really, and I am with you."

Tannah chimed in brightly. "I'm stuck with you either way, Scruffy. I couldn't leave if I wanted to."

Cendra looked at the three of them. They had a bond. She remembered how alone she had felt since she fled Esterby. Brandt was right—home could no longer be called home. She might not have understood herself now, but here at least perhaps there was hope. Hope that, even if she didn't understand, someone else might.

"You're right. I have to stay." She paused heavily. "I think perhaps ... I might *want* to."

Fionna let out a sigh. "Not without me, you won't. I have a duty to mind you. And if this is the course you're set on, I cannot merely observe anymore."

"One last thing," Brandt said sternly. "We're not keeping that fucking cat."

They rose with the sun the next day and began the return journey to Bellerenth early. They marched single file, each pondering the challenges they might now face having committed themselves to this path.

It was a short journey; less than an hour at a brisk pace. They were already nearing the town proper. Soon they could collect their fee and be on their way from this hateful place, leaving behind the bitterness of yesterday and the judgmental sneers of the people they had just defended.

Cendra stroked her sling bag where the hellkitten lay napping inside. As they made their way to their tents the night before, it had scrambled its way inside her satchel and curled itself up comfortably, quickly falling asleep. She hadn't had the heart to evict it, and now was in no hurry to reveal its presence to her companions.

As they strode into town, all eyes were upon them. The disheveled Scarbearers marched past them—bruised and burned, clothes and armor cut to ribbons. The silence was only broken by intermittent murmurings from the gawkers as they made their way up the steps of the town hall.

They hadn't even made it to the door before it was flung open and the mayor stepped out, undoubtedly having been alerted of their presence the moment they stepped into town.

"Is it done?"

Brandt stepped forward, licked his teeth, and spit. "Yes."

"Then our business is concluded." The portly mayor reached into his jacket and produced a pouch and flung it at Brandt. It hit him in the chest with an unexpected heft before falling into his palms. "Be gone, Scarbearers. May we never have need to call upon you again."

Brandt glowered at the little man as he retreated back into the safety of the hall before turning his attention to the pouch in his palms. He drew it open and looked inside. His eyes went wide.

"What is it?" Asked Fionna. "Did they short us?"

He looked back at her as a smile slowly crossed his face.

CHAPTER 10

THE QUIET IN THE EXTANT

The Feral Barrel, the sign outside had read. Though Cendra hadn't much experience with taverns or public houses, it was more or less what she would have expected of one, if a little ramshackle and improvised. An "extant," Brandt had called it—a refuge where Scarbearer Quiets could rest and resupply.

"They are typically run by Scarbearers. We are rare, and a great number of Scarbearers do not inherit traits suited for combat. They either try to carry on plying the trades they know or fill what demand they can to survive—and since most places will not have us outside of contracts, there is always demand."

Cendra cast her eyes across the room. While there were not many people here, at least not on this evening, *all* of them were Scarbearers. Around a table sat a group: A lithe figure with flowing red hair adorned with feathers was talking loudly, telling a joke or story. The Scarbearer looked perfectly normal until below the knee, where great hawk-like talons stood in place of legs. Next to her, a massive beast of a man with one great curled horn—the other broken off—guffawed and pounded his fist on the table as he drank from his own gilded and bejeweled broken horn. Their comrades chattered excitedly. Behind the counter was a little old couple, both very short with thick glasses and coarse, leathery skin. Their noses stuck outward and glistened under the sconces, glimmering wet over their elongated front teeth. They dutifully cleaned glasses and bowls, occasionally stopping to make little faces at each other or press their snouts together, and taking turns stirring a huge pot of stew. A handful of others around the room mingled, drinking, talking, and throwing dice. Cendra's forehead tensed. Her whole life, she'd understood that Scarbearers and magic folk were to be shunned, but the most abnormal thing here to her was how strikingly *normal* it all felt. Cendra was thankful for that. She was uneasy being out with this group without Fionna, who had opted out of this night of celebration to *give that damned cat a bath*, as she had put it.

It had been fifteen minutes and Brandt was already two-and-a-half tankards in. He had ordered drinks for all of them but Tannah, who sat sipping an imp's mint tea sweetened with ambercane. She had protested, of course, but Brandt was adamant that she was too young. He hummed a little tune as he sipped, flipping a golden Armine in his un-gloved claws.

Raure let out a little laugh. "A couple good drinks and you become a different beast entirely."

Brandt lowered an eyebrow at him.

"Sorry friend, an unintentionally poor turn of phrase."

"No offense taken," Brandt chuckled, "s'actually kind of funny. But no, it's not the ale." He poured another big gulp down his chops and set the mostly empty tankard on the table in front of him before letting out a mighty belch. "For the first time since I turned, I can relax a little. We can relax. We don't have to worry about affording our next meal or a roof to sleep under, at least for a while. As fond as I am of camping, I still appreciate a warm bed."

It was true. Though the job and reward may have been considered trivial for a hunt, the pay was still substantial enough to live well for a few weeks. They had divided the money evenly among them. Cendra glanced at the new coin pouch fastened on her belt. As alone and empty as she still felt, at least she could feel it in comfort.

Her attention turned from the pouch to the tankard of golden ale in front of her. The wine at Fionna's home was the only alcohol she had ever had; while it was available in Esterby, drinking had always been heavily frowned upon. She was not overly fond of the smell, which hung heavy in the air. She glanced at Raure, who had not touched his tankard, either.

Brandt cast a curious eye at them.

"What's the trouble? Not thirsty?"

Raure smiled at him.

"I do not partake, but do not mind me. I am more than happy to watch you all. I do believe it should be quite entertaining."

"Are you sure? We can stop if you're uncomfortable."

"No, it's fine. ..." he paused wistfully. "For some time after Anora and Flost were taken from me, I fell into the bottle. It was a dark place for me and I do not wish to return to it, but I assure you I am fine watching you all carouse. It is good to enjoy some levity after all we have endured of late."

Brandt was admittedly not gifted with words, but he did the best he could. He clapped a large mitt on Raure's shoulder.

"You're a good man, Raure." He glanced around the table, the alcohol taking a subtle but early hold. "You're all good people. I know this has seemed like a rough start, but even starting for folk like us is not easy." He raised his empty tankard toward them.

Brandt let out a surprised wolfish yelp as an even larger hand landed on his own back. In an instant he spun out of his chair, claymore in his grasp, ears back, and fangs bared.

"Whoa, easy friend." The horned man slowly raised his hands in front of him, still clutching his drinking horn.

"Koza! Back, you lummox!" Faster than anyone had noticed, the red-haired woman had put herself between Brandt and the horned man.

"Sorry, you'll have to excuse Koza. He's too friendly for anyone's good."

The giant of a man took a sip from his horn, waved, and smiled wide. "Didn't mean to startle you."

Brandt returned his sword to its sheathe on his back as a short growl escaped his maw. "No harm. It's just been a tense few days."

The redhead extended her hand toward him. "I'm Rukh."

He gripped her hand and gave it a quick shake. "Brandt."

"And this," she said, putting her elbow sharply in the horned man's gut drawing a quick *oof*, " ... is Koza. We're Rukh's Talons. What's your Quiet called?"

"Don't have a name yet. We're just off our first hunt."

"Sounds like cause for celebration! We're always glad to see new faces. We're unwinding between jobs tonight, if you all care to join us."

"Thanks, but we'll—"

"Yes!" Tannah's voice rang through the room as she was already out of her chair.

Brandt stifled a sigh. "Sure."

Cendra listened silently as they shared stories of their hunts: Rukh, whose legs were stolen by a rukh, so as recompense she stole its name; Koza, who long ago ran afoul of a capra, giving him his massive stature and grand horns; Aerich, a slender man with black hair, emerald eyes whose encounter with an akora left him with vertically slit pupils and patches of small mossy green scales on his arms, his forked tongue flicking the air. Next to him sat Ruprecht—he had an almost canine appearance not unlike Brandt, but was much shorter and narrower with ivory fur—flecks of what appeared to be snow falling like dandruff from his small vestigial vulpine tail. Finally was their mage, Savra, a tall woman with a dour face dressed in a padded cloth robe with auburn hair that fell in a long braid nearly to the floor—her domain was water and ice.

They were clearly experienced. They recounted battles with a cockatrice, a salamander, an anzu; her comrades listened with rapt attention, but Cendra could not help but feel lonesome. This life was still very new to her—she had no grand stories to share. She sank in her chair, an outcast of two worlds.

"If your posture gets any worse in that chair, you are going to fall out of it."

She was snapped from her contemplation by Raure's voice. All of them then turned to look at her.

"Sorry. Just lost in thought, I suppose."

Koza spoke up. "You look glum. Somethin' on your mind?"

Rukh gave him a light slug in the arm.

"Don't pry." She turned to Cendra. "Don't mind him, he does not understand boundaries, but his heart is in the right place. Don't feel you need to answer."

Cendra struggled. *Glum?* A gross oversimplification. Since the Scar manifested, she'd been adrift, powerless against tides she could not control.

"It's nothing. This is all still just ... very new to me."

"We get it. We were all new once. Adjusting to an entirely new life is no simple task, and a very lonely one. Look around the room, though. All of us at some point were there. Just remember that you're not as alone as it might seem."

Cendra's eyes welled for a moment before she fought it off. She simply nodded.

Brandt gestured to her tankard. "You sitting this one out with Raure?"

"Oh, I ... Well, I've only ever had wine, just the once with Fionna, and by the smell I get the feeling this isn't quite the same type of drink."

"Yes, it is quite different from wine. You'll find it's much stronger. It's alright if you don't want to. If you don't want it, I'll drink it."

She looked down at the amber liquid in the tankard. As she rocked it back and forth, it fizzed gently. She raised it to her lips and tilted it back with feigned enthusiasm. Too much enthusiasm, it seemed. The ale filled her mouth and her eyes bulged in their sockets. It was *vile*. She turned her head and spit it on the floor, coughing and gagging.

Brandt struggled to stifle a laugh. He had noticed how uncomfortable she was and didn't want to make it worse.

"Yeah, it's an acquired taste. Most people react like that the first time."

Raure had found a tattered cloth and went to wipe the ale from the floor, but as he looked down, a mischievous thought crept across his mind.

"Cendra—" he paused, giving wisdom a chance to temper amusement. It did not. "—if that had been flammable, *do you think you could have lit it?*"

"FIREBALL! FIREBALL! FIREBALL!"

They had all gathered outside, giving the building plenty of space in case of mishaps. Brandt had gone to purchase something stronger from the bar and returned with an ominous corked black bottle—across its otherwise-blank paper label were scrawled the unintentionally appropriate words "phoenix spit."

"Wow." Her eyebrows rose upon reading the label. "It's a miracle this exact situation hasn't burned this place to the ground before."

"Well, there aren't many fire Scars, so it's probably never come up," Koza chimed in, gracefully dodging the point.

"Why are we doing this again? You all know I can create fire from nothing, right?"

"Sure, but you don't breathe fire." Brandt looked down and puzzled for a moment. "Wait, do you breathe fire?"

"No. But this is still a terrible idea."

"Of course it is, but everyone gets to make a few of those every once in a while."

"That's a great example you're setting for Tannah."

Brandt frowned, then looked at Tannah.

"Turn around."

Tannah scoffed. "Not on your life, Scruffy."

Brandt looked at Cendra and shrugged.

"Alright, come on. Just one, just to see if it's possible."

She looked at the heavy black bottle in her hand.

"Fine. Just one. If this is anything like the last stuff, I'm never doing this again."

"Oh, it ain't like the last stuff," Koza chuckled, earning him another elbow in the stomach from Rukh.

Cendra huffed through her nose and uncorked the bottle. The aroma wafted up, its smell thick and heavy. Light hints of vanilla and ambercane with a heavy dose of something she imagined was normally used to clean saddles. She steeled herself, raised the bottle to her mouth, and, with a learned caution, drew the liquor into her mouth.

Cendra had learned that she was immune to fire—she and all she carried were protected by her Scar. She was not, however, immune to alcohol. She felt that the abhorrent brew was searing her mouth and establishing what she dreaded to be a semi-permanent foothold, flooding between her teeth and under her tongue. The ambercane and vanilla gave it a sweetness that might have almost been pleasant if it hadn't been added to a concoction only fit to remove varnish. Her face twisted and contorted in disgust and agony, but she held. Turning her head to the sky and pursing her lips, she forced the profane fluid into the air as a mist before setting it ablaze.

The little crowd made up of her comrades and their new friends cheered loudly, bathed in a cinnabar light as the fireball swelled for an instant and vanished to nothing. Cendra coughed and spit, desperately trying to expel the lingering taste from her mouth as they all gathered around her, patting her on the back and laughing loudly.

Koza howled in delight. "It's like making your own sunfire to attack the darkness!"

"That was a hell of a show, Cendra. Thank you for humoring us," Raure said with a smile.

"I'm glad you all enjoyed it, because that is never happening again."

Rukh let out a little giggle. "Hey, never say never. Sometimes fights get weird."

The laugh left Cendra's mouth before she realized it. As she watched them smile and laugh, she realized that these strangers had gone out of their way to make her feel welcome and included while she was at her lowest. It might have been in perhaps the most misguided and irresponsible way she could have imagined, but the intention was clear. She was grateful, for the moment.

Brandt let out a yawn as he stretched his arms.

"Alright, we've embarrassed Cendra more than enough for one night, and I've had enough drink that if I were still human I'd be dead. I think it's time I turned in."

They all agreed. Night had passed into early morning and fatigue was setting in.

"Yeah, I think we're all about spent. Where are you all headed next?" Rukh asked.

"Not sure. Hadn't really stopped to consider it yet."

Realizing they didn't have a plan began to gnaw at him. Brandt always had a plan; at least short term—until now.

"If you're looking for another contract, why not travel with us to Fairlight? We have an agent there, and if she hears about a team of neophytes taking down a hellcat on their first hunt, I'm sure she'll be able to find you a job quickly."

Brandt thought hard through the fog of his many drinks. They had only just met these strangers by circumstance at a watering hole on the side of the road. To travel with them to Fairlight on just a rumor of work? It felt reckless, but the offer was tempting. They had been nothing but friendly and given promise of easily found work—and he had had fun. They had all had fun. He scarcely remembered how to until tonight.

He looked around to his comrades.

"What do you all say? Does anyone have any other thoughts?"

He was met only with silence. He reached out and shook Rukh's hand with a smirk. "Very well."

CHAPTER 11
A WHISPER ON THE WIND

Brandt dodged swiftly to the left as the fetterclaw's stinger pierced the dry earth under him with a horrid crack. The point wedged itself between two stones, momentarily stuck. Brandt did not waste this opportunity, leaping on and wrapping himself around the segmented tail. He ferociously slashed and bit, but could not penetrate the stony exoskeleton with fang nor blade. Just as he made to dismount, the stinger broke free of the ground and sprang skyward, launching him headlong into the air. He came down with a thud some twenty yards away.

The impact knocked the breath from his chest. He paused in a crouch, watching from a distance as he caught his breath. Tannah's sparking bolts steered the fetterclaw's movements, keeping it contained to their chosen battlefield as Cendra whirled beneath it, a flurry of dagger and sword and flame. Raure's nimbleness kept the beast's focus divided; while he was loath to use the deadly gift of his Scar, the speed it bestowed upon him was staggering. It was difficult to follow him as he darted in and out of the fetterclaw's path, harrying it with his dagger. It had taken months of coaching, practice, and advice from their newfound friends, but Brandt found himself struck by their cohesion. Their skill had grown considerably in such a short time—they fought with focus and co-operation. While it had not been the precision his time in the military had led him to strive for, in the few months they had been working since their first job, they had developed rapidly. His thoughts fell back to Rukh. He would need to thank her for her part in getting them to this point. It had been little more than a week since they parted, but he missed them, her, already. They had promised they would meet back up. He promised himself he would see that it happened sooner rather than later. In his periphery, he spotted Fionna, also watching from a distance, her basalt arms folded across her chest.

As capable as they had become, he knew he could not remain out of the battle long. Fetter-claws were deadly and resilient, their venom capable of reducing a victim to a bubbling pool, with a stone hide that could turn all but the mightiest of blows. They were among the beasts that only ex-perienced teams of hunters would tangle with, and the healthy reward for their contracts reflected this. The trio was holding their own, but that would not last if he lingered with his thoughts.

Brandt rolled on to all fours and drew a deep breath, then another. He sprinted back into the fray.

They had begun to garner some renown for their effective—if unorthodox—approach. Their last contract had been with the village of Crestvale to dispatch a colossal frostquill. The Quiet to take the job before them met a grim fate; it had cost the lives of three Scarbearers to only just repel the monster.

The stands had swirled with rumor and speculation as Sunfire—the name they had taken upon themselves after the fireball incident—engaged the beast; the crowd that had been expecting flash and flourish instead looked on as the team had measured the beast slowly and methodically, dancing in and out of combat. The spectators grew restless; in their eyes they beheld a quintet of inept neophytes engaging a monster that would surely be their demise. They were unaware that Sunfire held their gifts in reserve, for Brandt had purpose. On his signal, a great pillar of flame burst under the Frostquill, drawing it headlong toward Cendra. She smirked as the trap was sprung; as the beast stepped on the mark Cendra had dug in the dirt with her toes, a cage of lightning sparked to life, arcing violently around the beast among the darts and knives Raure and Tannah had been strategically placing in the ground.

At a shout from Brandt, a gap in the cage briefly opened; he and Raure sprang to action. Brandt leapt onto the Frostquill's neck, pounding its head with the pommel of his claymore as Raure produced a flask from his bag, waiting intently. A handful of blows to the temple and the beast's head crashed to the ground. The pair drew thick scarves over their faces as Raure, with a mighty swing, shattered the flask across the beast's muzzle. The lightning cage blinked out of existence and the pair scattered frantically as the dense yellow fog spread from the splintered bottle. A massive groan escaped the throat of the frostquill as it struggled to rise, only for its legs to fail. It fell to the ground once more, its chest rising and falling with the breath of deep slumber.

The crowd was silent for several moments before rising into a riotous roar; what they had expected to see was a killing, but killing is simple. What they had witnessed instead was unprecedented. Upon receiving their pay and purchasing a heavy wagon, instead of partaking in the festivities, Sunfire had simply vanished, hauling the beast deep into the wilderness.

Cendra had reflected on Sunfire's first hunt together as they all unchained the sleeping frostquill, far in the wood where its hunting would be unlikely to lead to human encounters. Fionna and Brandt rolled it off the cart as gently as they could manage. Raure smiled as he watched the creature breathe deeply, patting Brandt on the back. Brandt's dour expression had belied the ember of compassion within him; Cendra saw him smirk as he looked back at the peacefully sleeping creature. There would be no death on this hunt.

Lark Falls, a quaint, peaceful riverside village, was now abuzz with people. The small amount of fame they had garnered had drawn a crowd to this hunt; so many, in fact, that it bore resemblance to the carnival-like hunts of the more prominent Quiets. The smell of popped corn, street meats, and other various types of festival foods filled the air. Above the noisy chatter of the crowd rose the occasional call of a street peddler.

While Fionna was pleased with the success Sunfire had found, the logistics of protecting onlookers from the dangers of the fight had become a concern, one they had not previously had to consider. In most Quiets, containment was the primary function of a Quiet's Caller, as their talents were often most suited to summoning a barrier from a distance. It was fortunate their Quiet had two members that could fight at range in Tannah and Cendra, but both lacked experience and could prove a liability.

Cendra was best suited for containment in Fionna's estimation, but Brandt had assigned the duty to Tannah. He had argued that Tannah should bear that responsibility as she was the Caller, where Cendra was far more capable of direct combat. He was not wrong; Cendra had proven to be swift and strong, invaluable when faced with a powerful foe. Fionna was growing tired of her counsel falling on deaf ears, but she let Brandt have his way.

The fetterclaw rushed past Fionna, far faster than its immense size would suggest. She leapt back, shielding the hellkitten as best she could. The kitten, Aska, had grown quickly since they had adopted him. Though he was still nowhere near adult size, he was still too large for Fionna to completely shield with her own body even if he had been content to hide behind her—and he was decidedly not. He lurched out at the massive beast, just missing with his razor sharp flaming claws. Luckily, the fetterclaw scurried right past them, barely aware of their presence.

The massive fetterclaw made to impale Cendra with its deadly stinger. She deftly rolled out of its path as the great barb slammed into the ground just where she had stood. She wheeled around on her heels and raised her hands with a roar, calling up flame from the ground below the lethal barb. The fetterclaw recoiled in agony as its stinger crackled in the searing column of flame, releasing a deafening screech and flailing madly away from the font of pain. The reprieve was only momentary, and Cendra was not prepared for how quickly it renewed its assault. The beast lunged for Cendra as she tumbled backward on the ground, so near that she felt the rush of air as its pincers surged toward her throat, when it was met with a crackling azure blast. Cendra sat frozen for a moment as the great scorpion hissed and turned its attention to Tannah. There was no doubt in her mind that Tannah had just saved her life, but at great risk; while they had managed to seize the fetterclaw's focus, Tannah's lightning was an ill match for its stony hide. She shrieked as the beast surged in her direction.

Brandt was sprinting to catch up to the fray as the unnervingly quick fetterclaw darted around the battlefield when Tannah's scream reached his ears. Reaching its hind, he fell on his haunches and slid beneath the monster, between the massive legs that pulverized the earth beneath it with each brutal step. He sprang skyward, interposing himself between Tannah and the beast's chittering mandibles. With a mighty roar, he flung his greatsword end over end at the monster's eyes. The long blade found its mark; black blood sprayed from the eye socket as the long blade buried itself deep within. A victorious smirk danced across Brandt's muzzle, but prematurely—it faded as the massive crystal pincer closed around him. The breath was pressed from his lungs as his claws tried in vain to find purchase. His legs swiped futilely at the air as he struggled to breathe. Held helplessly aloft, he watched as the monstrosity's tail coiled, the stinger aimed for his gut. He closed his eyes and waited for the venomous lance to pierce his flesh.

With a thunderous crunch and an agonizing yelp, the pincer loosened and dropped Brandt unceremoniously to the ground. Before him stood Fionna, her clenched stone fist dripping with blackened blood. Jagged cracks wound through the beast's stone hide as it backed away, fleeing to the south, safely away from the spectators and the town.

Fionna stood over Brandt watching the monster retreat. As she sighed and looked down, she saw his wolven face staring up at her, smirking.

"Well, you weren't getting anywhere with that thing, and I couldn't smell that food for another two hours while you all chased your tails. If you'd listened to me, we'd be eating already." She sneered at him as she offered him a hand.

"How many times do we need to have this out? They need to learn their roles. Flexibility is fine, but without dedicated responsibilities every fight will be pure chaos. Besides, I knew you couldn't keep watching." Laughing, he reached for Fionna's hand but was interrupted when Aska jumped on top of him, burying his face in Brandt's neck. "Get this damned thing off of me!"

Fionna left him there, struggling to avoid Aska's affection.

"Don't play with the cat long. I need to get some of that corn before the vendors pack up."

"I'm serious, Fionna! I hate cats," his voice cracked under the strain of a stifled laugh.

Carts and tents lined the stone-paved main street, all offering something to the hordes of people walking by enjoying the novelty of the day. This street was normally quiet, with a handful of shops in which you could find the normal food or wares one would need for everyday life. Today, however, you could find nearly anything, from small trinkets to large ornate artworks, from candy to exotic meals, and much more.

The townspeople were not the only ones enjoying the festivities. The members of Sunfire, for the most part, were enjoying themselves as well. They couldn't help but feel a little like the stars of the show. While caught up in the excitement of the day, many of the townsfolk seemed to ... not forget, but ... set aside their fear and dislike for Scarbearers, if only for the day. Cendra, in particular, was having a great time. She felt at ease, like she was back home, before her transformation.

"Don't buy into this." Brandt was sitting on the ground, leaned against the wall of the livery, tossing a knife into the dirt. "They'll want us out of town tomorrow."

"I didn't think you cared if they liked you or not." Cendra joined him on the ground.

"Would I rather they liked us? Sure, but I don't care if they do or don't. What I can't stand is this," he motioned to the people passing by them, waving, smiling, some even thanking them. "None of this is genuine. It's all fake."

Looking around at the festivities, Cendra took Brandt's meaning.

"Yes, but look over there," she gestured to a young boy who stood at his parents' knee, staring in amazement at Brandt. "He has been smiling at you since I sat down. It's not fake to him. He sees you as a hero. I know of course his parents may teach him to fear us, but the seed of acceptance has been planted. It's moments like these that will eventually lead to widespread change."

Brandt looked at the boy, considering Cendra's words. He smiled at him, and watched as the boy's face lit up.

"Hmph. Perhaps."

"Still, you're right. Our welcome will wear out soon. That kid isn't the only one staring, though—there's a man over there that has been watching us, and something about him is ... off."

Brandt's ears perked up, "Where?"

"He's right over—" Cendra gestured to empty space. "Oh, he's gone."

Brandt looked around for a bit, sniffing the air. Seeing and sensing nothing, he turned back to Cendra. "I'm sure it's just one of those Whispers. There's one in every town."

"Whisper ... ?"

"Well yeah, not everyone harbors hate for Scarbearers; even we have our patrons. Some of them follow their favorite hunters from town to town, almost obsessively."

"Have you tried the salted sweetleaf?" Tannah asked exuberantly as she, Raure, and Fionna, walked up.

"Who with a functioning mind would salt a sweetleaf?" Brandt asked.

"That's what we thought, but it is amazing! They cure and smoke it like salt pork. It's sweet and savory, you have to try it. Come on, we will take you there."

"Hell, I'm game. We were about to leave anyway. Cendra spotted a Whisper."

"Oh? Grey beard?" Fionna asked.

"Yes," Cendra's eyes were wide as she responded. "How did you know?"

"I saw him earlier. He was following us right after we arrived from the fight."

"I suppose we were to just go on all day, unaware?" Raure asked, his voice carrying no small hint of sarcasm.

"I saw no need to disrupt the mood. He was just an odd fellow, but he didn't seem to mean any harm. You know how these Whispers are. They just want to be around us, for whatever reason."

"I suppose you're right, no reason to spoil the merriment. Let's go get these two some sweetleaf and see what else this festival holds." Fionna could tell Raure had been annoyed, but just as fast as it had come it was gone—she admired his unrelenting positivity. Raure bounded up the street on Tannah's heels with a little skip in his step.

The salted sweetleaf vendor had drawn a sizable crowd. She had introduced a new treat to the world, and it seemed everyone in town had heard and wanted to try it. Cendra watched Brandt fidget as the team waited in line for what he had eloquently described as "too long," but once he tasted it, his tune changed rapidly.

"Armine's *tits* I'd almost stand in that line again."

As they carried on down the street, they all kept an eye out for their admirer, hoping to avoid any awkward encounters, but as the afternoon wore on, he had yet to make another appearance.

"I think, perhaps, we were hasty in our judgment of our shy friend," Raure chimed. "We'd have seen him multiple times by now if he were a Whisper."

"Yeah, I think you are right," Fionna said, relaxing a bit.

Brandt was not as easily convinced.

"We should go collect our pay and prepare to leave. Night will be closing in soon, and I want to camp out of town."

"The treasurer was back at the children's cart races when we passed by, he may still be there," Tannah said, turning around to look for him.

Johann Purceval, the town treasurer, was a timid man, but was oddly not afraid of or in any way unkind to the Scarbearers. He saw them walking toward him at the cart races and left his spot at the side of the finish line to meet them.

"I assume you are ready to settle up?" he asked.

"If you are ready, we'd like to be on our way," Fionna replied.

"Surely, I'll just need to find the mayor. She will need to witness payment. It's just a formality." He beckoned them to follow. "I'm sorry to see you go so soon, have you secured another job?"

"Not yet, which is fine, I think we are all due a little break," Fionna was anxious for some down time.

"Agreed," Raure added, as the rest of the group nodded.

"Well, the mayor should be close by. I'll go and find her and we will meet at my office. It shouldn't take more than twenty minutes."

Brandt nodded, "We will wait for you there."

"How is Cendra?" Raleth had asked Helene this question every day.

"She is coping. You should write to her, she'd like to hear from you."

"I think it would be best to give it some time. There's no need to hurry. All of this silliness will end, she will return, and things will be back to normal. You will see."

Helene smiled and nodded, then headed off to meet with the abbot.

Something stole Raleth's attention. A noise behind him. He turned just in time to see the barghest's eyes. That was all the time it needed. He felt the pressure building in his head. He lost consciousness before blood erupted from his ears, and he collapsed. The barghest pounced, tearing the meat from Raleth's lifeless body.

"How long has it been?" Tannah asked.

"Too long." Brandt was getting irritated. It had, in fact, been nearly an hour since they had left Johann to meet at his office. The shadows were starting to get long and an uneasy feeling nestled in his gut.

"Maybe we should go find them," Cendra offered.

"Wait! No, I am here. I'm sorry, I was held up and was trying to get here as soon as I could," Johann called as he came running up.

Brandt grunted his displeasure, "Where is the mayor?"

"I'm afraid she could not make it, she has asked that I invite you back tomorrow to discuss the terms of the deal."

"The terms have already been discussed. The job is done, all that is left is for us to collect the money due," Fionna was now as irritated as Brandt.

"I'm afraid she does not share your opinion that the job is done," Johann nervously stammered.

"Of course it is done, the fetterclaw is gone. That was the job." Brandt was growling as much as he was talking.

"I don't disagree with you. In fact I was late getting here because I was trying to convince her that we were permanently rid of it. She is not easily swayed."

"We were planning to be gone tomorrow!" Brandt had his finger in Johann's face. "You tell your mayor—"

"—that we will remain here to ensure it does not return," Raure interrupted. "We stand by our work and want our clients to be satisfied."

Johann pressed his palms together and bowed in a combined "Thank you" and "Goodbye." He was clearly relieved. His fright at Brandt's ire was plain on his face, and he was eager to get away.

Brandt struggled to contain his fury, but saw the wisdom in Raure's move; escalating the argument would have been fruitless at best. He turned and started walking.

"Let's go make camp."

As they departed for camp, an uneasy feeling crept over Cendra—the feeling of once more being watched.

"It's just horrible." Helene looked back at Raleth's coffin as she and Abbot Larson left the funeral. "He is the last person I would have imagined losing his life to one of those things."

"Yes, and now this second attack has all of Esterby in a frenzy." The abbot shook his head as he watched frightened town people hurrying back to their homes.

"Has there been any word from the Conclave?"

"As a matter of fact," Alderman Breoghan interrupted, having just come into earshot, "We came to an agreement just before poor Raleth's funeral. We have sanctioned the commission of a Quiet. In fact, I've already sent word to Lark Falls. As I understand it, that is where your Cendra's team is and they are staying there for a few days."

"My Cendra?!" Helene's excitement was quickly eclipsed by doubt. "Do you really think that wise? She was forced out of town, the people here surely don't want her to return." While she longed to see her daughter, her fear of the consequences weighed heavy on her.

"Helene, I thought you'd be pleased. I'm taking a chance that this might be an avenue toward acceptance of Cendra. Maybe this could lead to her possible return, if only for short periods of time." Alderman Breoghan reassured her.

Helene's heart skipped a beat, "Do you really think that is possible?"

"It's no certain thing, mind you, but surely it could not hurt to try. Don't get your hopes up, though. We don't even know that she would come back to help the people that ran her off."

"I do." Helene dismissed the question.

Breoghan smiled, "Excellent."

"Shit!" Brandt threw his mallet across camp and splintered it against a tree. His second stake had snapped; he had been taking his frustration out on them as he set up his tent. Work stopped at the commotion and everyone stared at him.

"I can finish this," Raure picked up one of Brandt's stakes and began to drive it into hard ground.

"Don't. I don't need any help."

"It seems to me that it is these poor stakes that need help," Raure smiled. "Go have a seat and stew a bit."

Brandt rolled his eyes, "Thanks." He took a seat by the fire that Cendra provided.

"I don't understand why you are so upset. We've dealt with this type of client before," Fionna prodded Brandt.

"Don't," warned Tannah under her breath as she moved past Fionna on her way to the relative safety of the other side of the camp.

"Why? Are you afraid of the puppy?"

The joke caught Brandt off guard. A short snort escaped him.

"There we are," Fionna laughed. "What is the problem? We've waited for pay before."

"It's not that, it's that damn Whisper. He wasn't acting right; he wasn't clamoring to meet us, he just ... watched. It's suspicious. It's *grating* at me."

"I'm no Whisper," the old man stepped out from behind a thicket several yards away from the clearing.

Brandt was up and in his face in an instant.

The man, chuckling, lifted his hands to the sky, "Easy. Easy. I am not here for trouble."

"Then why are you here?" Brandt asked, still nose to nose with the stranger.

"I'm here for her," he replied, pointing at Cendra.

Raure and Tannah stepped in front of Cendra, showing the stranger that he couldn't take her without a fight. Brandt let out a long low growl as Fionna stepped to his side.

Laughing again, the stranger put his hands down and strolled over to the fire. He made himself at home, despite the openly hostile attitude of his hosts.

"It's not like that. My name is Raythent. I'm here at your request," he said, warming his hands. "Is there tea?"

"What do you mean, by 'at your request'? I've never heard of anyone named Raythent," Cendra asked, stepping between Raure and Tannah.

"I received word from a mutual friend. A man named Porter."

CHAPTER 12

RIDDLES IN TWILIGHT

They watched in silence as the silver-haired man set a stone over the campfire then placed a tin teapot on it. He swept a long gray lock from his eyes behind his ear, then from his pack he gathered a stack of small tin tea cups and six silken pouches.

Cendra's frustration was growing.

"You said you had information about me?"

"Yes. For starters I know that you were raised in a place with manners. I have information, yes; but I also have tea—and I don't know about you lot, but I am *parched*."

"And how, precisely, would you know where I am from?"

Raythent shot her a stern glare.

"Well, I can sense that you seem to be in a hurry. I suppose that is fair." He placed one hand on the side of the teapot. Within moments, steam began to rise from the spout, and he lifted it from the fire. "You could say that I was an acquaintance of your parents." She could see his eyes soften with sorrow. "Their passing was a tragedy." He placed one of the silken pouches in each of six cups and passed one to each of them. "And yet, they live on through you, Scar or no. I have lived a long life and have made many friends. Nobles and knaves, Scarbearers, wizards and common folk—and through them, I heard of you. Quite the reputation you're building. You seem to have adapted remarkably well even without understanding the nature of the beast that inflicted your Scar."

Fionna spoke up. "When we asked Porter for help, we were actually hoping to find someone who might know—"

"And I may well be the best you will get. I have seen many a Scarbearer in my time, but I believe you'll all agree that our Cendra here is quite unique. Based on what you know, what have you guessed thus far?"

"Well, the scales limit the possibilities to the reptilian, I'd assume," Fionna mused.

Brandt piped up. "All the fire definitely narrows it down a lot. Not a basilisk, hydra, akora, kappa ..."

"What monsters are reptiles that use fire?"

Brandt paused to think for a moment. "Only ones I'm familiar with are salamanders and chimaeras."

"Unlikely," the old man said. "A chimaera is only part reptilian. If it had been a chimaera, no doubt there would be more here than just scales." He walked over to Cendra and held out a hand. "May I?"

Cendra nodded.

He brushed the hair away from her face.

"And notice the color. A salamander's skin is like coal: coarse, dull, and jet black. A chimaera's serpentine tail ranges from muddy brown to a deep, woodsy green. Cendra's scales are red as rubies and have a glossy sheen."

They all looked at Cendra. They agreed, and were at a loss.

The man folded his hands and rested his chin on them. After a short pause, he spoke again.

"Have you considered a dragon?"

All of them laughed—all of them apart from the old man and Cendra. Brandt noted their expression.

"Oh gods, you're serious, aren't you?" He stood. "Dragons are a myth. They don't exist; they're either stories people tell their children to scare them into behaving or the ramblings of madmen, and even the godsdamned *lunatics* haven't claimed to see a dragon in the last fucking century! Not to mention, every story ends the same way. There are no survivors. There are no bearers of the Dragonscar because there are no dragons. If the dragons ever were, they are long gone, and all that would have remained of their victims are bone and dust."

They all muttered their concurrence as the old man sat silently drinking his tea—all but Cendra. She was ill at ease. She couldn't decide what she hated more—being the focus of this attention, or what the attention directed at her was centered on. Yet something else gnawed at her mind. She remembered the stories Brandt spoke of. She'd heard them from childhood friends while playing around town. Helene frequently told her stories and fables—but now that she thought of it, never once had Helene told her stories of dragons.

"I realize how implausible that sounds, but the case stands. The way her Scar has manifested—the scales, her fire and strength—they preclude the possibility of any other creature we are aware of. Dragons may be myth; it certainly fits the symptoms, does it not?

Brandt scoffed softly. Cendra pulled her amulet from under her collar and rubbed it between her fingers to calm her mind.

The old man took notice of the amulet for the first time. He gave her a quizzical look. "Where did you get that?"

"It was my mother's." She looked mournfully at the stone in her hand. "It's all I have of them now."

He walked toward her. "May I have a look?"

Cendra pulled back momentarily, then held it aloft, still around her neck. He held it gently in his palm. The gold of the pendant glimmered in the firelight, clean and untarnished. Set in this dazzling but seemingly delicate frame was a large red stone, faceted in a near-teardrop shape. The large, vibrant gem was inconceivably clear and within it swam a softly glowing wisp, like a flame dancing in a pool of scarlet.

His brow furrowed and his face grew pale as he dropped the amulet gracelessly back to her chest. His eyes met Cendra's.

"What you have there is unique. I do not mean rare. You carry around your neck a treasure without measure; its value cannot be quantified in gold or titles—and for some, even in *souls*. What you have been given is not merely a memento, but a dire responsibility. Trade it for nothing, relinquish it to no one and guard both it and yourself well, for the few who know what that stone truly is may well be willing to kill you all for it."

Cendra lifted the stone and gazed into it and waited for him to continue—in vain.

"Is that all you're going to tell us? A crackpot theory about dragons and then to tell me that we're all in danger because of a piece of jewelry? What's so special about this?"

"It has a name. That stone is the Heart of Armine. It is said it is a stone born before creation, a priceless artifact of a time long past. You are already in danger for merely possessing it; knowing more could potentially make you a danger to yourself and countless others. You know all you need to know. Protect it with your life."

Tannah was puzzled.

"Armine? Like the gold piece?"

"Armine like the *goddess*. Our coinage was named for them long ago—the goddesses Armine, Eduni, and Ilona."

Cendra knew them well. Her entire life until the Scar had revolved around them. She had avoided thinking about them ever since she fled Esterby. What was she to them now? What was the sum of her life until now if they would abandon her for something beyond her control? She scowled at the amulet, then turned her gaze to the old man.

"If it's as important as you say, why don't you want it? Why don't you take it and protect it?"

He chuckled. "Dear, I am an old and withered man. How could I possibly safeguard such a treasure? Shall I beat off my attackers with my teapot?"

Cendra watched as he mocked a few fencing jabs with his teapot and made swishing noises with his mouth.

"Surely. You can't be older than, what, late forties if my eyes don't lie?"

"Old or no, your sword form is pretty good," Raure snickered. Brandt choked back a laugh.

Raythent set his teapot back down.

"Well, young lady, for all you know perhaps I am cursed with youthful countenance—or maybe I'm just a coward. I will leave it to your imagination. Either way, I want no part of carrying that stone, so no, I will not try to take it from you, nor do I have any desire to."

"Remarkable. After all you've told us, I know even less now than before." Cendra stood gruffly. "Thanks for all the help. I am going to sleep."

"It has gotten rather late," Raure chimed in, stretching lazily. "We should all probably consider turning in."

Brandt nodded.

"Aye. Let's hope Lark Falls finally sends our fee early tomorrow. I'd like for us to move on soon."

The silver-haired man stood.

"If there are no objections, might I make camp with you here? It's a bit late for me to be making the trek back to town."

"Fine," Brandt grunted, already making for his tent. "As long as you have your own gear."

Sleep would not find Cendra, at least not yet. She lay awake, staring at the amulet laying next to her bedroll. Its soft red glow danced across the walls of her tent. She reflected on the months since she left home. The glow flickered across the scales on her cheek, sending a crimson shine into her eyes.

She ran a finger over the Scar where the scales parted. *Scarbearer.* Every time she heard the word, saw the fear and hate in people's eyes when they saw her, or even saw her own reflection, resentment boiled in her chest. *What have I done to deserve this?* Her mind seethed. Her whole life she had tried to be good—*had* been good, certainly as good as anyone else in Esterby. The worst that could be held against her were perhaps a few childhood pranks with the other kids around town. She had lived by the laws of the Conclave and the prescriptions of the Triune—and they cast her out. She hadn't come by the Scar through her own actions. She didn't choose it.

She didn't *choose* it. *Choice?* The thought raged around her skull like an unfettered bull. Had she *ever* had a choice? She had never considered it back home, as it was simply how lives were lived. She turned her face into her pillow, burying it hard. As she cast her mind back, she felt her whole life had been preordained. Who she was, what she would do with her life, who she would marry—hell, if she even *wanted* to marry—all of this had been decided for her. Her opinion was not asked, and as her mind burned with racing thoughts, she doubted it would have even been considered. She brought a fist down hard onto the cold ground and desperately choked down a sob. Her whole life she had been robbed of choice, and now she had come to realize that she *hated* it.

Cendra emerged from her tent to sit by the dwindling fire and was surprised to see the silver-haired man sitting silently watching the dying flames. She sat on the ground next to him.

"Sorry, I didn't expect anyone else to be awake."

"No need to apologize; I'm just watching the embers. I find it comforting, in a sense."

As she watched them pulse red and black, she felt she understood. Cendra sighed.

"I'm also sorry that I was short with you earlier. I am grateful for what insight you were able to provide."

"No offense taken, lass. You've had a very hard go of it lately, especially having come from a place of such comparable comfort."

"If I'm honest, I'm not sure it was much comfort anymore."

He sipped tea from his cup and chuckled softly to himself.

"Fair enough. I'm sure you would agree it was at very least *easier*. These have been trying times for you, indeed—though, I fear, not as trying as times to come. I know it will not come easy, but you really should rest while you can." His face went somber. "Though I wish it were not so, you all will most assuredly need it."

Morning had come far too quickly for how long it had taken to drift to sleep. Cendra woke to the sound of talking outside her tent. She lazily rubbed the sleep from her eyes. A flash of light caught her eye, a reflection of the morning sun off of a single facet of the scarlet gemstone resting against her nightshirt. Her thoughts returned to the warning the old man had given her about the stone, but what was she meant to do with it? Until now, it had just been an heirloom, her last remaining keepsake from her parents. Could it really be as important as she was told, and, if so, how was she possibly meant to safeguard it?

She pondered the thought as she laced up her boots. She was surprised how fond of them she had grown. While their new lifestyle had not made them rich by any means—and even if it had, not many shops would openly do business with Scarbearers—she had spent a considerable amount on them. They were comfortable and durable, a dark walnut brown with a brilliant polish, lacing to the knee where a cuff wrapped around. She remembered her old shoes back home, how they cramped her feet and hurt her toes; walking in them was at best uncomfortable. But now, in her boots, she felt agile.

She had just started tying the second when her tent opened unexpectedly. Brandt peered inside, stern.

"Cendra, you are needed. Quickly."

His tone was low and urgent. He had never addressed her this way. Her concern grew as she emerged from her tent. A young man carrying a satchel stood with the rest of her companions as Brandt gestured for her to come forward.

"Again, to her." Brandt's brow was furrowed so low she wondered how it did not dislocate his nose.

The courier unfurled a parchment and began to read.

"On behalf of Lark Falls—"

Brandt gave him a light cuff on the back of the head.

"No, you dolt, the second one."

The courier stammered and produced a second missive.

"O–on this day, nineteenth of Tornal, 1453, a contract is extended to the heretofore unnamed hunting party of Brandt et cetera von Lusenbil III and company. Services to be rendered include—"

Brandt growled menacingly. "'Services to be rendered' would be pretty godsdamned obvious, wouldn't they? Out with it, whelp!"

The reedy young man flipped nervously through a handful of pages before continuing.

"'Contract shall be satisfied upon extermination of known magical creature listed in this document identified within the territory of the city. A further bounty shall be rewarded on extermination of further magical creatures yet unidentified in accordance with classification. As the above-mentioned servicer has intimate knowledge of the city, contract shall be considered exclusive until such time as the threat becomes unmanageable or it is deemed a response is not forthcoming. This contract is time sensitive—please respond with haste.' There's a bit of postscript here that seems to have set your man off. 'Cendra—return home. Whether the people here know it or not, we need you. The city guard cannot fend much longer, and more seem to be coming. Please come home. Signed Alderman Aethan Breoghan, City of Esterby.'"

"It seems it's time for a homecoming, Cendra," Brandt grunted. "Good thing he brought Lark's payment. Everyone, gather your gear—we set out immediately. Old man, you're on your own from here." Brandt had turned to address Raythent, but, to their surprise, he and all his things were already gone.

CHAPTER 13
HOME IS WHERE THE HEART IS

Brandt had been on edge since they departed Lark Falls. Too many strange happenings in such a short time for his taste; the foreboding hung around him thick enough he could swear it had a scent.

"Something is off." Brandt broke the hour-long silence that had fallen over the group deep into their trip toward Esterby, but the group remained silent, trudging hastily onward. "No, stop." He paused momentarily to give articulation to his thoughts. "Why Cendra? Why would this town call back their own exile? That doesn't happen."

The question was half rhetorical, but Raure offered perspective, "I take your meaning. That said, perhaps to their mind it is preferable to contend with the devil-you-know."

"Sure, but if you've angered the devil, you don't invite him in. What's been troubling me, though, is how they knew we were still in Lark Falls. Helene knew we had a job there, but she couldn't have known from my last letter that we were held up,"

Fionna had been considering the question silently, since the word had come from Esterby. She had not been ready to verbalize the nagging feeling that this was some sort of trap set for Cendra. Now that Brandt had broached the subject, she couldn't stay quiet.

The hesitation irritated Cendra. There was no debate to be had; no time to spare. Her family and friends were in danger. Once the thought had set up shop in her head, it evicted all others. The conversation had caught her off guard.

"What are you suggesting? That there is no threat at home?" She paused briefly, awaiting an answer that would not come. "Why? What purpose would there be in that?"

"Maybe that stone around your neck is the reason," Tannah chimed in, giving voice to her suspicions. "Doesn't it strike you as odd that some strange man gives you some cryptic warning about that thing, and not a half day later, we are suddenly called back to your hometown? I'm with Scruffy, something isn't sitting right."

Cendra clutched the stone tightly. "He's a deranged old man! Are you all actually buying into that nonsense?"

She was frightened for her mom, she felt like she could not get home fast enough, but now, her new friends seemed to be doubting that they should be going back there. Heat was building up around her. The smell of hot dust filled the air, like the first fire of fall in her bedroom hearth. Everyone slowly backed away from her.

"Nonsense or not, Tannah has a good point. We need to be cautious. We could be letting our imaginations get the better of all of us. I hope we are, but, Cendra, we have to be prepared for anything." Fionna spoke quietly and calmly, she had learned how to calm Cendra down over the last few months. Cendra had a powerful temper, but she was very practical and intelligent. Sound, logical reasoning could bring her back down, as long as it was not shouted at her.

Seeing Cendra relax, Brandt brought them all together.

"We cannot plan for what we do not know, so we need to know as much as we can. What we need, Cendra, is the best description of Esterby that you can give us. I want every detail, the layout, the buildings, the people, everything you can think of. Fill us in during the trip. If you think you're telling us too much, it's not enough. When we arrive, I want us *all* to feel like we're coming home."

"How did they get inside the outer walls?" Breoghan was frantically shepherding people into the inner gates.

"The guard on the western tower said the gate spontaneously combusted," Abbot Larkin shouted from across the street. He was writing names of people as they passed.

"Spontaneously combusted?!"

"Yes. It seems the gate was engulfed in flames in an instant, reduced to a pile of ash in mere seconds."

"Which guard? Surely they were shirking their duties and have made up this ridiculous story to cover their ass."

"There are other witnesses that confirm their account."

"When this is all over, I will launch a full investigation. People are dying in the streets and someone needs to be held accountable. A barghest pack within the city walls! It will not stand! How is the count?"

Larkin looked at the people waiting to enter, and back at his list.

"We are going to be short at least a dozen."

Breoghan inhaled sharply, "As many as that? With *three* other gates?! Gods! I'll finish up here, go get some help setting the hall up for the care of the wounded." He motioned for the clipboard.

Larkin rushed the clipboard over to him and ran toward the gate.

Helene held her breath as she peered through the gap of the cupboard door. It was the nearest place to her when two barghests crashed through the door of the apothecary, eviscerating the shopkeeper and at least one customer. There must have been around four or five other customers in the shop at the time, if she remembered correctly. It all happened so fast she could not be sure who had gotten out, who was still in the shop, or who was already dead.

She could see both barghests through the gap. They were massive black wolves with icy blue eyes, their fur so dark it seemed to swallow the light. She had heard stories about them, but had always assumed their size had been exaggerated. If anything, they had been undersold: taller at the shoulder than the display shelves they walked by— the very same shelves she could barely see over without standing on her toes.

A whimper came from behind the counter, no doubt it came from the young boy Helene had seen shopping with his mother no more than a few minutes earlier. The two monstrous wolves keyed in on the sound and stalked toward their prey. Pressing against the cupboard door lightly with her shaking hand, she began to slowly open it. The hinge squeak might as well have been a trumpet sounding as the barghests turned and growled at the cupboard, ears folded back and fangs bared.

The larger of the two looked back at the smaller. It seemed almost as if they conversed silently before the second turned back toward the child and the first started toward Helene.

She had not had a plan when she tried to leave the cupboard, but if she had, this would not have been it. She could scarcely contain her fear, holding her hands over her mouth as the giant wolf approached her. She shuddered as its muzzle pressed against the gap she had been watching through. Helene could feel the rush of air as it inhaled sharply. The air was still for just a moment while the beast processed the scent. It then snorted and let out a growl so furious and low it almost sounded like a flurry of beats on a deep drum.

Helene readied herself. She had little doubt that this was the end, but she would not go easily. She loaded herself like a spring; as soon as the door was penetrated, she would bolt out. Maybe—*just maybe*—she could get by the wolf and get away.

A long, terrifying howl pierced the tension from somewhere in the distance. Both barghests turned their heads to it, then, in an instant, they were gone. Helene cautiously slipped out of the cupboard. Confirming that the beasts were gone, she ran back to the counter. The scene broke her already-troubled heart. The child had found his mother, who had been nearly torn apart, and was holding her head in his lap. He rocked back and forth, sobbing.

"I'm sorry, Mommy. I'm so sorry. ... I love you, Mommy!"

She knelt down and held him.

"She knows, child. She knows."

"At last count, there were twenty-seven injured, forty-two unaccounted for. Tower guards report that the barghest pack is reformed in the north-west park." Gareth's face was contorted in both fear and narrowly contained anger.

Breoghan paced the floor of his chambers as he processed the report.

"Have the north and west inner gates shut, and get a search party for missing and wounded in the southwest section. Also gather blankets, linens, and medicine for the injured. The apothecary is in the southwest. Get the medicines there. Blankets and linens from the homes. Make it fast, they will not stay still long."

Gareth seethed. "I will see that people get the supplies gathered, but I will see those monsters dead. Those *things* ... " His smoldering eyes glistened. "They took my boy." Gareth turned to go, but hesitated. "There's one more thing. Alderwoman Trelana is among the missing."

Breoghan stopped, and leaned against his desk.

"Find her. Go! Now!"

Following Gareth out of his chambers, he went into the main hall to check on the injured. He found Abbot Larkin tending to a man with a particularly vicious bite taken out of his thigh.

"Lorek Fairbury. How is he?"

Larkin pulled Breoghan out of earshot.

"The bite is bad, but the real concern is that the Fever has already set in. We are about to have a hall full of deathly sick people. Almost everyone in here has been directly wounded by the beasts."

Breoghan shook his head.

"Make them as comfortable as you can. I have men out searching for the missing, they are also out for supplies and medicine."

"I saw Gareth; Helene is among the missing." Larkin's voice cracked.

"I'm sorry, friend," he placed a hand on Larkin's shoulder, "If she's out there, we will find her. Chin up. These people need what optimism and good cheer we can muster. We all do."

Larkin nodded, "Any word on Cendra's Quiet?"

"The scouts have not returned, but I would expect the first to return within the hour."

"I hope so, but I don't think they will be prepared for ... *this*."

"We couldn't hope they were. They're a very clever group, though. Like I said, chin up." Breoghan smiled reassuringly, and headed outside to assess the scene.

Brandt halted abruptly.

"Someone approaches from the front."

"I see no one." Raure argued after scanning the horizon.

"Their scent has been getting stronger for some time now. I imagine they will be on the horizon soon," he sniffed the air. "There is only one."

"They must be coming from Esterby; we aren't far now." Cendra stepped ahead, and watched the horizon. "Wait—I see someone." They all watched intently as the figure sprinted in their direction. "That's Namolis! She's on the city guard."

Namolis came quickly to the group, heaving for breath. She had clearly run long and hard for some time.

"I was sent to hasten you, as things have become dire in Esterby. A pack of barghests have broken through the outer wall."

Cendra stood in stunned silence, her mouth agape.

"Barghests ... How many?!" Brandt was keenly aware of the dangers that they posed.

"Seven, as I understand it," Namolis gasped out between ragged breaths.

Brandt recalled what he could of the city from Cendra's description. "Have they barricaded the people in the city center?"

"They had started the process as I was leaving, it should be done by now."

Brandt glanced at Cendra before asking the next question, "How many dead?"

"I do not know. I saw at least a handful and several injured on my way out."

"Triune ..." Cendra gasped and turned to hide her face from the group.

Brandt nodded to Tannah.

"Get Namolis some drink and honey comb." He turned back to Namolis. "We will need to hurry. Can you keep up?"

"I would not have been sent if I couldn't."

"Good. Cendra, I know how you must feel. For now, you will have to bury it. The best we can do is get there as quickly as we can carry ourselves." Brandt's voice was kind but stern.

Cendra straightened her back.

"Let's go."

As Helene, the child, and the final guard passed through the gate, they were met with cheers. Behind them the gate slammed shut, startling the child. Helene took a knee beside him.

"You are safe now, Rylan. I will keep you with me until we find your family." She stood facing the gate.

"Helene! Thank the gods you are alright. We feared the worst." Abbot Larkin had come to see that she made it back. Getting no response from her, he asked, "What is wrong? Are you harmed?"

"I've ... I've never seen it shut." Helene stared at the gate in disbelief.

Larkin followed her gaze back to the gate.

"Yes. I'm not sure they have ever been closed. I am sure that they will not remain closed for long. Who do you have with you?"

Helene set her worry aside and turned her attention back to the boy.

"This is Rylan, he and his mother were in the apothecary when the barghests came in."

Larkin began to look around for Rylan's mother before realizing what must have happened.

"Well, Rylan, who can we help you find?"

" ... My dad." Rylan winced as he answered, and rubbed his side under his arm.

Larkin and Helene glanced at each other.

"He said he wasn't hurt."

Larkin bent down, "Rylan, you must tell us. Are you hurt?"

"Just a scratch."

"How did you get the scratch?"

"The mean dog scratched me."

Helene's heart sank. By nightfall, Rylan would develop the Fever, and by morning, he'd most likely be dead. At the very best, he would survive the Fever, and be an outcast.

"Let's get you cleaned up and find your father." As the abbot stood, he sighed and shook his head at Helene.

"The outer gates were all left open in the hopes that the barghest pack would leave," Namolis explained as they walked through the wide open western gate. Inside, they found dead, and a few poor souls already suffering with the Fever. They gave each of them water, giving them what comfort they could in what were most likely their final moments and promising to get them help as soon as they cleared out the barghests.

"It's very quiet. Perhaps they have already gone?" Tannah glanced warily around for any sign of movement.

Brandt lifted his nose to the air.

"They are most assuredly still here, and they know we are, as well." He sniffed the air again and growled. "I know this pack."

The words had no more than left his lips before his body began to change, his limbs elongating with a series of grotesque crunches, his hackles standing on his spine.

Fionna nodded to Namolis.

"Let them know we are here, and to keep the gates shut until we give you the all-clear." To the north a lone howl broke the silence of the city. "Go now!"

"Gloves off, Raure." Brandt grunted out through the agony of the change.

"I would rather wait until it becomes necessary. ..."

"Now. Trust me." His glaring yellow eyes flashed with purpose.

Raure nodded hesitantly.

"One." Raure recognized the weight in Brandt's voice, unbuckling the gauntlet from his left arm and tucking it in his belt. He looked at his palm and distanced himself further from the group.

"This barghest pack is known to me. The alpha of this very pack bestowed my Scar; I recognized its scent the moment we stepped in the gate. They are strong, fast, and deadly. Barghests are not unlike wolves in many ways. They hunt with purpose, for food or territory. ... but something is amiss here. Barghests do not seek conflict without purpose. Something has triggered them ... starvation, disease, I don't know. This erratic behavior means they are unpredictable, and thus all the more dangerous. Keep your wits firmly about you. Watch yourself and your neighbor, and if the chance comes to take one down do not hesitate—for they most assuredly will not. Don't let fear slow you. I know what they are capable of, but I also know what we are capable of. Use your heads and each other. These barghests have killed their last—let's see to it."

He turned toward the north and crouched down, his body was a taught spring, ready to be released. Aska strode to his side, mirroring his pose. Brandt nodded, turned his head to the sky and warned the barghests with a deafening howl.

The barghests proved much faster than Cendra had anticipated. Over the past few months, she had improved greatly in her control of flame, but these wolves made it plain that she was still a novice. By the time she had produced a flame in their path, they had already sprung past or had changed directions in a flash, as if anticipating it would be there.

She shifted her fight strictly to defense, maintaining columns of fire around herself with gaps for monitoring the battle. She wished she had the ability to keep all of her comrades shielded in flame, but only she and Fionna were impervious to fire.

For his part, Brandt was gaining ground in battle with a single wolf. They were evenly matched in speed, but Brandt was seasoned and clever. Every lunge from the beast earned it a measured swipe from Brandt's own claw or blades; blood glistened on them in the moonlight. Tannah and Raure stood back-to-back, working in tandem against two barghests, holding them at bay. The smell of singed fur and the sound of pained yelps swam in the air, Tannah's bolts searing their hides as brief touches from Raure's ungloved hand sapped their very essence. Fionna was perhaps faring best as her basalt arms gave her a natural advantage; every fang and claw met with naught but stone. Aska, though still young, had grown much since they had adopted him. Measured against the barghests, he was still quite small, but his natural command of fire earned his foes much pain. Cendra momentarily found herself envious of the young hellcat's instinctive affinity for the flame.

Get it together, Cendra. Everyone's lives are on the line and I'm jealous of a damn cat.

She weighed her situation. The lone barghest that had made her its focus was proving little more than a nuisance to her. Upon every attempt to breach her defense, it reeled back, burned by her columns of flame. She feared, however, that if she extended her concentration to assisting her team, her barrier would weaken or fail. This was compounded by the disconcerting fact that she could only account for *five* of the barghests.

"How are you faring, young one?" Raure called, dodging swipes from his young wolf as he checked on Tannah behind him.

"Fine, as long as I can keep some distance between us. Those claws are sharp!"

"The claws are certainly a problem—they are keeping me from getting in close. I need to lay a hand on her for more than a mere moment, but I cannot find a way in. I did manage to get a blade in her. Perhaps if I can get another in, and hopefully a little space, we can switch?"

"I'll keep mine on its heels, just say the word and we will rotate left." Tannah sent a powerful lavender bolt at her wolf, backing him up.

Landing another throwing blade into the howling beast, Raure called out. "I could do with a bit of space here, Cendra dear, if you can find a moment!"

With somewhat less warning than Raure would have liked, a ball of flame burst on the ground before Raure, sending the barghest back.

"Now!" He yelled at Tannah, and they quickly turned counterclockwise around each other, switching opponents.

Tannah lit the two knives with long arcs of crackling electricity, electrocuting the yelping barghest. Its smoking form collapsed to the ground, spent. Tannah turned to help Raure.

"I don't suppose that would work twice."

Raure let out a dark chuckle. "I'm out of blades, I'm afraid."

"I'll get you an opening." Tannah moved to flank the beast on their left.

Raure mirrored her motion until they were opposite each other, the snarling barghest between. Tannah saw her opening and lobbed another azure bolt into the beast's backside. With a great yelp, it spun to face her. The trap sprung, Raure jumped on the wolf's back, taking handfuls of its hide in his pallid gray hands. His black veins swirled with green wisps as the barghest struggled frantically for several agonizing moments. Its flailing grew sluggish and lethargic as its life drained away and, at last, the mighty barghest fell.

Persistence had paid for the barghest stalking Cendra. The momentary disruption in her focus in assisting Raure had opened a gap in her flaming defense, wide enough for the beast to swipe through and flay open her back with its massive claws. She fell to her knees in agony as her flesh ripped open. She rose to her feet as the snarling barghest circled the pillars of fire. Rage flashed across her eyes as the columns of amber flame pulsed and surged with a fierce white heat. With a roar of pain and fury, she sent the columns spiraling wildly outward. The barghest wheeled around, attempting to flee, but far too slowly. The beast was engulfed in the raging inferno. The flames dissipated, leaving naught but a pile of ash and bone.

She stood over the ash pile, reeling from the fresh wound on her back. She rolled her shoulders and drew a deep breath before remembering they weren't contending with the full pack—others were still out there somewhere. She quickly re-conjured her blazing cage and glanced frantically around the streets.

"Brandt!"

The prowling alpha, laying in wait, capitalized on the chaos and struck. Her coal fur bristled in the moonlight, her eyes golden pools of deadly intent upon a sea of black. As Brandt contended with the smaller barghest, she was on him in a sable streak, as if a ray of emptiness had cut through the space between her and her prey. Fionna's desperate cry had not faded before the beast had pinned him to the ground from behind, its crushing jaws clenched around his shoulder, thrashing madly.

Instinct drove Cendra as she ran. Her heels pounded the cobbles as she charged forward, bolides crackling in her palms. With all the force she could muster, she launched twin blazing orbs forward in a blinding flash.

They detonated in a searing flash. Behind the flare, Cendra was stunned to see Fionna, who, having delivered a knockout blow to her barghest, had run to help Brandt as well. She had, in the last moment, interposed herself between Cendra and her mark, shielding Brandt from the orbs.

"Cendra, stop! Brandt is still under that thing!"

Fionna wheeled around on her heel, storming with her shoulder low and plowed into the side of the smaller barghest with a grisly crunch as its ribs caved under the unyielding force of her charge. It tumbled down the street, but would not stay down. It was on its feet in an instant and, before Fionna could reclaim her balance it lunged, taking her to the ground. Fionna guarded her throat with her arms, the beast unable to find purchase in her mineral hide, but the barghest was too close for her fist to gain momentum for any meaningful impact. They wrestled, locked in an impasse.

Brandt lay pinned under the alpha, his shoulder still locked in its jaws as his free arm struggled desperately to reach his claymore, which lay on the street just beyond his fingertips. For all his resilience, he could feel the bones in his shoulder starting to give under the crushing force of the alpha's maw. He grit his fangs. This monster had already robbed him of his life once;

he would not allow it to do so again—if only he could reach his blade.

Cendra was in full sprint, but the distance was too great. The danger of using her flames was too great, and with only her blades at this range she was powerless. She looked around desperately for Raure and Tannah but they were in no better position, too far from the struggle and with too much metal for Tannah's magic to not imperil them further.

Cendra's heart lurched. She was about to watch Brandt die, she was certain. A scream boiled in her throat but, before it could take form, Aska surged past her, his burning footfalls leaving embers in his path. With phantasmal speed he bore forward, launching himself with paws wide, claws bared, with a desperate roar. Aska's claws caught the alpha barghest's shoulder and whipped him around onto her back, where he plunged his fangs deep into her nape. Under the swift assault of piercing, searing pain, the barghest released Brandt's shoulder with a yowl that rattled the cobblestone beneath them. It thrashed erratically, madly, attempting to dislodge the burning hellcat. Aska's fangs lost their hold and sent him whipping around the barghest's throat, where he was met with a ruthless blow from her monstrous swiping paw. Aska soared through the air, slamming into the wall of an aromatics shop. He fell to the ground. Aska struggled to rise, but his legs had no strength. He collapsed to the street.

The alpha stalked toward Aska's motionless form. Towering over the beaten hellcat, the barghest snarled as she watched his chest rise and fall weakly. Satisfied that the hellcat was no longer a threat, she turned her focus back to Brandt. She rushed at a blistering pace, her fangs eager to pierce his throat.

A sickening squelch as flesh gave way. The sound bubbled through the air grotesquely as the barghest's head rose, pressed upward by Brandt's massive hand buried deeply in her neck. Rage burned in his eyes, his form even more swollen and stretched as fury poured through his veins. He pressed up from the ground, raising the barghest skyward by the throat as it thrashed and gurgled.

"YOU WILL NOT KILL ME AGAIN." With a bellowing cry that reverberated through the guts of his comrades, Brandt closed his fist, crushing the barghest's windpipe.

The party watched on in stunned silence. At the death of the matriarch, the last of the barghests abandoned its fruitless struggle with Fionna and fled down the street in the direction of the gate. Fionna stood and joined the group as Brandt fell to his knee, exhausted.

"Saved by the godsdamned cat." He placed his palm on Aska's side, ensuring he still drew breath.

The little hellcat was battered, but alive. "You brave little asshole." He gave a gentle scratch behind the ear as he exhaled his relief. "There will be no more fighting for you today. Thank you."

Raure slouched his shoulders as he released a heavy sigh. "Let us fetch help for the wounded."

As the gate opened before them, the Quiet was met with hearty cheers. They walked side by side through the gate. Cendra's heart was in her throat as she saw Helene running toward her. They met in a tight embrace; Cendra wincing at the pain of her wound but, as Helene tried to draw back, Cendra pulled her in tighter.

"Cendra! Oh Triune, my Cendra! I'm so glad to see you safe! Are you alright? Are you hurt?" Tears escaped her eyes, running quickly down her worry-lined cheeks.

A warm smile broke across Cendra's face.

"More than alright, Mom, now that I know you're safe." Cendra choked back a sob. So many were wounded or dead; tears would have to wait. "I've missed you so much."

"Oh, she is far tougher than she looks."Abbot Larkin was walking toward Cendra, arms outstretched to embrace her. Cendra smiled at him and stretched out her arms.

A blasting rush of wind. Her eyes clenched shut as warm mist brushed her face. Screams of terror filled the night sky. When her eyes opened, the abbot was gone. She wiped her face with a trembling hand.

Blood.

CHAPTER 14
THE GRAVE IN GRAVITY

Helene's mouth moved, but Cendra heard no words. What entered her ears was drowned by a thrum in her head as if deep underwater, her mind racing to process what she had witnessed. Helene cried and screamed, spattered with blood and trying to pull Cendra away. To where and for what purpose escaped her. Her mind spun wildly.

Cendra fell to the ground—or, rather, she was tackled, she thought—as a blur passed overhead. She lay in the dirt as her senses slowly returned. The abbot was dead. Something had killed him—something fast. The thrum faded as a voice drifted into focus.

"It's a gryphon! Cendra, You need to pull yourself together!" It was Brandt. He had tackled her out of the beast's path as it swooped from the sky, clutching her face between his hands with a firm shake. "Cendra, listen to me! It's you and Tannah—that is it! The rest of us are the south end of useless until it's grounded! You've got to bring it down! Are you hearing me?!"

Beyond him, she beheld the chaos that was unfolding. Panic-stricken people fled in all directions, trampling one another as they lit for shelter. Some stood locked in terror, their wide eyes turned to the sky. Cendra watched helplessly as the gryphon plucked a young man from the street and carried him aloft, pierced through the chest and shoulder by massive talons. The youth thrashed and screamed to the height of his ascent, whereupon the gryphon released its grasp, dropping him unceremoniously to his death on the cold stone below.

The gryphon had not been hunting in hunger, nor for sport. It was not defending its territory; this was a rampage driven by a madness beyond her ken. It slaughtered indiscriminately, just as the barghests before it. Cendra did not understand—but knew she did not need to. The gryphon would not cease its attack, so she would have to end it herself. Fully recollected, she nodded with determination.

"Just get it on the ground, that's all we need. Cendra, you can do this!"

She looked back at Helene, still latched to her arm and wailing.

"Mom, go. We have to stop this thing. *I* have to stop it. Get these people inside!" She pulled her arm away, then paused and looked back. "I love you."

Helene could only watch silently as Cendra strode with Brandt out into the emptying street, tears streaming down her face. The child she had raised had grown brave and strong. She choked down the sobs and called out.

"Cendra!"

Cendra paused and looked back.

"I love you. Come back safely."

Cendra smiled warmly and turned back into the night. Helene's breath came in uneven huffs as she steeled herself, then began the work of organizing people to guide the survivors to shelter.

Brandt and Cendra crouched low as they made haste to rejoin the group. Tannah projected wild, raging arcs of electricity with Raure and Fionna acting as spotters, chaining them between spires and weathervanes as she tried to connect with the darting gryphon. Azure bolts flashed against the night sky but the gryphon eluded them all, diving out of sight beyond the abbey.

"It's too fast." Tannah's shoulders fell, sapped of energy. She paused to rest while the gryphon was out of sight. "All I'm managing is to aggravate it. I hope one of you has a plan!"

"There is no plan beyond getting it out of the air, whatever it takes." Brandt's tone had lost its force; he was at a loss.

"There's no time to think." Fionna pointed the beast out, fast on approach from the east. "It's coming 'round again."

Tannah's eyes widened, shock draining the blood from her face.

"That's not ... " Her voice trailed away.

"What?"

"That's not the same gryphon!"

A horrid shriek rang through the streets as the falconlike beast swooped low on dark wings of shimmering blue and green, its talons and paws folded back, beak wide in a shrill cry, lethal focus in its eyes.

Brandt's eyes followed the beast through the air as it passed overhead, unblinking in bewilderment.

"Look!" Cendra pointed beyond the spire of the abbey, where the first gryphon emerged in the sky on the far side, its ravenlike features silhouetted against the moon.

"Circle up, face out! Cendra and Tannah, opposite each other!" At Brandt's word they gathered in formation. Brandt snarled as he watched the winged predators circle overhead. "This is madness—*this doesn't happen*. Gryphons hunt goats and deer in the wilds, they never raid settlements—and now, here, *two* of them."

The streets had nearly been emptied, Helene and her assistants ushering the last of the survivors into the safety of the ironstone abbey.

With the crowds dispersed, Brandt knew they would be the remaining prey for the winged death above. He briefly considered splitting the group to allow focus on a single gryphon, but they were too mobile. By remaining together, they controlled the zone of attack, perhaps the only advantage available to them.

The raven-colored gryphon dove from the sky, talons primed, targeting Tannah, who had been pummeling it with whips of crackling energy. Instead of the satisfying feel of penetrating flesh, its talon shattered against the basalt hide of Fionna's arm as she leapt between the shrieking gryphon and its mark. With a shriek of agony, it pulled itself back up into the sky.

"Cendra!" Helene had emerged from the Great Hall and descended the steps, calling out to her. "Everyone is inside!"

Her shouts caught the attention of the falcon gryphon; it swiftly abandoned the party for easier prey. Cendra looked on in terror as the beast streaked toward her, but Raure was already in flight. The beast was nearly upon her as Raure threw his dagger, his aim never truer. It pierced the gryphon's leg under the knee, the pain forcing it to retreat once more to the sky.

"You have to get inside! We must repel the beasts, but I will see that Cendra is not harmed!"

"Raure!"

He felt the talon enter his back and burst through his chest before Tannah's scream had even reached his ears. He watched Helene's face distort with fear as the claws closed over his shoulder and sank into his torso, and finally the ground fell away as he was hoisted into the air. Higher and higher they climbed as the beast soared skyward, its coal-black wings beating furiously as sparks and fire burst in the air around them. Raure's senses slowed and his mind cleared; if he could get a knife into this gryphon as he had the other, Tannah would have a reliable conduit at which to channel her magic. Blood bubbled from his throat as he coughed. His remaining dagger was sheathed on his hip, under his left arm that flailed from the shoulder, helplessly trapped in the gryphon's grasp. With his right, he grasped for the blade. It came free from the sheath and tumbled from his hand as the gryphon thrashed, plummeting to the ground below. He could feel the gryphon's grip loosen—he would be dropped to his doom. He closed his eyes.

"Papa!" Raure chuckled heartily as he and Anora watched Flost run around them, arms spread wide, pretending he could fly.

He closed his teeth around his glove, in his mouth the tang of blood and leather.

The sun shone down on a grassy field. He and his beloved Anora lay under the sunlight on a blanket as Flost gathered flowers, singing softly to himself.

His skin burned as his jaws pried the still-buckled leather gauntlet from his arm.

The three of them sat together by the fire, soft moonlight pouring through the window as Anora read Flost a story of faeries and elves.

"Anora ... I am coming home."

Through agony and tears, Raure reached out and latched on to the gryphon's leg at the ankle, clutching with a strength known only to those at the edge of death. The beast shrieked in anguish; it rolled and tossed in the sky, desperate to shake his grasp—but Raure would not relent. His veins swirled violently with virescent magics, channeling the beast's very anima from its body. The gryphon released its grasp in desperation attempting to drop its tormentor, but still Raure held firm. They careened wildly through the air as the beast flailed. The emerald light swirling through Raure's arm swelled and pulsed as the beats of the gryphon's wings weakened, its cry fading in the night. It thrashed no more, its wings lifeless at its sides. No sound remained but the wind.

They cried out helplessly from the ground as the pair plummeted from the sky. Tannah and Cendra made to run for him, but Brandt grasped them by the shoulders. His voice was low, but soft. "No. It's too dangerous; one yet lives." They turned to him to protest, but saw the tears welling in his wolven eyes. "We will go to him. After."

Brandt steeled his nerves and locked his gaze on the surviving gryphon. As its shimmering wings of blues and greens pounded the chill air, he spotted a glint in the moonlight; the glint of metal protruding from the beast's leg.

"He's done it! Raure's dagger is still in it!"

Tannah's gaze fixed on the knife, her eyes and palms hissing and crackling. She slammed a tremendous cerulean bolt into the dagger as the beast released a stunned shriek, crashing into the ground. Fionna, Brandt and Cendra charged forward, laying into the beast as it stumbled to its feet. Cendra's flame coursed through her dagger and longsword, leaving blazing wounds. Brandt was a cyclone of steel and fang, tearing through feather and flesh. Fionna's granite fists slammed into its hide and deflected strikes from its razor-sharp beak. It was not enough; the gryphon reared back and with several mighty beats of its wings the trio were pushed back and the beast took once more to the sky—wounded, but enraged. With several kicks of its hind leg the long knife dislodged, falling to the street with a metallic clatter. It ascended high into the sky and unfurled its wings under the moonlight. Once more, it dove.

Cendra's heart pounded slowly. She thought of Abbot Larkin, his kindness and acceptance. She thought of Raure, his wisdom and heart. They were gone.

No more. Her blood was molten steel in her veins. Her face relaxed, her eyes narrow, her brow low with cold fury. All thoughts melted away, all save one; all that remained was deadly purpose.

Her eyes tracked the beast's shrieking descent. The air shimmered and hazed around it; wisps of smoke and tiny embers danced in the wake of the plunging gryphon. Her muscles tightened. From deep within, a bestial roar poured from her throat as the very air burst around the gryphon, so thunderous it staggered even Brandt. Vermillion light flooded the streets as the vast flare engulfed the gryphon, lost from sight in the blinding light of the inferno. The group dove clear as it slammed into the cobblestones with a gruesome crash, a roiling ball of flame and melted flesh, its feathers burned to a wet, black smoke. They watched in astonishment as it burned away, a terror of the sky now a blackened corpse on the street.

Their foe disposed of, their attention returned to Raure. The group sprinted to his side.

The gryphon had struck the ground first, Raure's form sprawled atop it. The gryphon was depleted to a lifeless husk. Raure's chest rose and fell weakly.

"Raure! I tried so hard! I'm so sorry; I tried. ... " Tannah sobbed as she fell beside him. The rest of the Quiet joined her at his side.

"I know, little arc," Raure whispered through shallow breaths. "You did so well. I am proud."

"I'll go get help!" Cendra turned to leave, but Raure stopped her.

"There is no use, child. I am spent." Raure gasped weakly as pain surged through his broken body.

Tears streamed down her face as Cendra kneeled by him, resting her hand on his chest.

"Thank you for saving my mother ... for saving us. Thank you. For everything."

Fionna smiled down at him as her eyes glistened.

"It has been an honor."

"Take care of them, Fionna."

Brandt laid a hand on his friend's forehead, "Is there anything we can do for you? Some herbs to ease the pain?"

"That time has passed, my friend. The pain will pass soon. Thank you for rescuing me from solitude. I had not known how desperately I had needed it." He smiled. "Good boy." Raure's eyes drifted to the moon. "Anora ... " He passed into the night, a smile on his face.

Brandt hung his head. For most of his life, he had known battle. He had lost friends and comrades. Tonight, for the first time since before he could remember, he wept.

Tannah shifted as she felt a brush on her arm; a little purple flower swayed in the breeze, growing through a cracked cobblestone. As she gazed down, the emerald glow bled from Raure's arms into the ground. Flowers pushed up through the earth between the cobbles where the green glow poured, spreading from where his body lay. They bloomed and spread around their fallen friend. With trembling hands, Tannah slipped Raure's satchel off his body, taking it over her shoulder, clutching the strap tight as they stepped back in reverence.

The silence would not last. Stalking from the shadows through the night, the final barghest struck. It slammed into Brandt, sending him toppling to the ground as it surged past. It turned with blistering speed, building momentum to finish Brandt before he could produce his weapons.

With the sound of rushing air and a handful of thunderous beats, a horrid screech rent the night like the air itself crying out in agony as a titanic gout of flame engulfed the barghest, incinerating it mid-stride. The conflagration cut a vast swath across the street, setting buildings ablaze as the barghest crumbled to blazing coals, tumbling end over end.

Brandt looked at Cendra in utter bewilderment.

"When did you learn to do that?" The sound of beating continued, louder.

Cendra's eyes were wide, fixed firmly on the sky. Her voice quaked. "That wasn't me."

Scales glittered red in the night, bathed in firelight; colossal wings blotted out the moon. Its tremendous cry shook the rooftops as it poured its volcanic breath into the black sky.

"Dragon!" Fionna's voice warbled with fear and disbelief.

Cendra had never seen Brandt afraid; or at least not in any way he would show. The horror now was plain, his eyes wide in awe, his jaw slack in terror.

"Get to cover!" Brandt seized Tannah and threw her over his shoulder as he burst into a three-legged sprint. "The Hall! Now!"

Flame fell from the heavens around them as they ran, a storm borne of Hell itself.

"Split up! Don't give it a single target! Randomize your path, but get to the Hall!"

They diverged at the corner, ducking down the alleys and streets of the intersection. As they scattered, the dragon tracked Cendra as she wound through the alley. The ground behind her burst in explosions of flame and debris. Having made it into the Hall, the rest of the Quiet watched from the door, urging her on.

"This isn't right. Nothing about this is right. It's like it's not trying," Brandt had been muttering to himself, but Fionna had heard.

"What do you mean?"

"That's a *godsdamned myth* out there. A dragon! It disintegrated that fucking barghest as if it had been tied to a post, and Cendra couldn't hope to match its speed. It should have killed her twenty times by now! This isn't a hunt. ... it is *toying* with her."

Fionna watched as the gouts of flame pounded the earth. They harried her, but always just short or wide of their ostensible mark, alternating sides each time.

"I ... I don't understand. You're right, but why ... ?"

"Why anything?! No sense is to be had here! A pack of barghests terrorizing a village for what, *sport?* Gryphons, only ever encountered in the wild, plucking people off the streets? Now a nightmare, a *fucking legend* soars in the sky above us!"

Cendra fell through the abbey door and laid on the cool marble floor, trying to catch her breath.

"Get her on her feet and away from the door! One breath from that thing could reduce us all to ash!" Brandt started pushing onlookers back further into the hall as Fionna and Tannah took Cendra's hands and pulled her to her feet. "We need to think. We can't linger here, there are too many openings. Mighty as the walls may be, this building will not protect us."

Tannah clutched Raure's satchel silently, trembling with dread.

"Going out that door with that *thing* in the air is a death sentence. We will have to wait until it leaves." Fionna struggled to maintain composure; as much for her sake as her companions'.

"We cannot assume that it will." Brandt looked around the hall, weighing how long they could survive within its walls.

"The tunnels!" Helene's mind raced back to Cendra's flight from the city. "They wind through caves underground, emptying outside of—"

Helene's voice trailed to silence as the dancing light of the fires outside gave way to a shadow falling over the door. The survivors turned their gaze outward. Cendra's breath came in ragged heaves, her heart sinking into the pit of her stomach as she looked through the doorway. Filling its blackened frame, an eye—colossal, amber, and unblinking—stared back at her. This was no fleeting dream, but the terror of reality. No, not merely reality—a memory, returned once more from the depths of her past.

The eye fixed upon her, twitching as its focus lurched up and down her body. Her hand reached to grasp her pendant. *Gone.*

The eye narrowed in a furious glare as a bellowing snort shattered the stained glass windows of the Great Hall. The eye rose away from the door followed by a tremendous roar that quaked the floor beneath their feet. A mighty blast of wind through the door as its wings gave fearsome beats, pounding the air as it heaved its gargantuan body aloft. The beating continued, fading steadily into the night until it dwindled to nothing, leaving no trace but the fires that had burned in its wake. The dragon was gone.

Fear released its hold on Cendra as she burst through the door. She clutched at her neck again, but the stone was well and truly gone. She cried out into the night as if challenging the dragon to return, but was met with only silence.

CHAPTER 15
THE HOLLOW IN THE HOME

Two days and nights had come and gone since what would be known as the Battle of Esterby. Tower sentries never ceased scouring the horizon, but no trace of the dragon was to be found. Surviving scouts led by the intrepid Namolis searched the fields and around the city, even venturing some measure into the wilds beyond. Though Brandt had lent his heightened senses to the search, not a single scale was found. As Cendra watched the sentries high in their towers, she surmised that their vigil would not soon end.

For every three of the city's survivors, one more was dead, in the throes of the Fever, or on the list of those yet unaccounted for—a list that bore the names of all three Alderpersons the Conclave comprised. For two sleepless nights, Helene toiled, tending to wounded, organizing groups to clear rubble and repair homes, advising the city guard now bereft of leadership. She wanted nothing more than to be with her daughter in the aftermath of the nightmare they had endured, but with so many lives ended or upended, she could not be idle. For her trouble, Helene had found herself proclaimed interim Steward of Esterby; or rather, the responsibility had fallen on her.

To the considerable task of stripping the wreckage and shoring up walls, Fionna imparted her might. She and Helene worked side by side with the people of the city, from tailors to bakers, carpenters to potters, nobles to beggars; they worked through day and night to restore order to their home.

As the sun grasped westward on the second day, they had nearly cleared the rubble and ruin, but rebuilding would take far longer. Helene walked the floor of the Great Hall, checking in on the sick and wounded. Of the forty-two wounded who had been found, the Fever had already claimed the lives of thirty-seven, their still bodies covered by sheets as the five that yet clung to life groaned on their makeshift beds. Tannah's hands worked in a trance, pulling herbs from Raure's satchel, grinding them with water into a poultice to soothe the victims' pain. Not a word had crossed her lips in the two days that had passed. Helene looked over the wounded. Their faces were known to her, smiling at her on sunlit mornings as she walked the streets. Their names hung in her mind as she watched them wail in their beds, sweat beading at every pore. In his bed tossing in fitful fugue lay Gareth Prentish, his countenance twisted in pain, his shirt soaked in sweat and blood.

Helene had remembered his hate, the antipathy in his heart as he hunted her daughter through the tunnels beneath this very Hall, the curses he had spit on her name. Deep within her, for a brief instant she flared with anger; she felt he deserved his fate. Shame washed over her as her senses returned. *No. We are better than this—we must be. No soul deserved this.* She gently wiped the sweat from his brow with a damp cloth.

"Mother?"

Helene turned from her toil to see Cendra and Fionna standing near.

"You sent for us?"

Breoghan's chamber lay in disarray. Parchments, books and scrolls were strewn across his desk and floor, the drawers turned out as if by a desperate thief. A chest and safe beyond his desk sat open, their contents long since removed.

"With the Alders missing, we began searching their records," Helene began. "Treasury records, deeds, ancestry documents; anything that would be of use in the recovery." She led them around the desk to the back of the room where the door to Breoghan's private library stood. "We found much of what we needed in Stonlek and Trelana's libraries; enough to start providing assistance at least—but what we found here is ... *peculiar.*"

Opening the door, she led Cendra and Fionna inside.

The library was in a similar state to the office proper; parchments lay unfurled across the floor, draped over open tomes, dangling from the edges of tables. The bookshelves had been cleared, but with purpose, it seemed. The books had been removed and stacked high on the floor in several high towers; the space once theirs on the shelves occupied by a staggering assortment of curious contraptions and trinkets. Alembics and phials, rods and scales, mirrors and lenses: these and other strange curios were lined neatly upon the shelves. A box on the corner of a nearby desk contained a pile of faceted stones of vibrant color and exceptional clarity. They bore a semblance of the stone Cendra had possessed; beautiful though they were, they were a crude echo by comparison.

Cendra pulled a stone from the box and ran her thumb over its faceted edges.

"Why would he have all this stuff?"

"I don't know." Helene looked to Fionna. "I thought they might be of particular interest to you. Some of the tags and documents we've found in this room lead us to believe at least some of them are magical in nature."

Fionna stood over a stack of books. She gently ran a stony thumb through the dust on the cover.

"These are old. *Impossibly* old." She glanced around the towering stacks, across the tools and devices littering the room. "I'm not sure if I'm more confounded by 'why' he had them, or '*how*'."

"Breoghan had no will; no records indicate any surviving family or heirs. I know you enjoyed studies on similar relics with Barret and Shyla. We will hold his possessions for a fortnight; hopefully by some miracle he returns, but as it seems now. ... " Helene released a deep sigh. "After that, the city bequeaths them to you. There is only one condition—if you find anything that can help this city, please let me know."

Fionna turned her gaze from the collection of curiosities to Cendra.

"This is important, Cendra. The rest of you will have to go on without me for now; there could be something here."

Helene's heart sank at her words.

"Oh, child. ... "

"We have to take Raure back to Dulainn." Cendra's words were soft, but insistent. "He died to protect this city, after we promised to keep him safe. He died to save you, the only family I have. It's only right that we see he is returned to his."

Helene fought back tears. "Will you come home after?"

"Mother ... Of course I want to be near you; since I left I've wanted nothing more desperately than to come home. But it has changed—or perhaps I have. This city is not home for me; it hasn't been for some time. It can't be, until I have answers. My Scar, my parents, the stone ... The answers are with that dragon, wherever it has gone."

Helene's voice flushed with fear and panic. "Cendra, if you go hunting that monster it will be the death of you! You can't—"

Her voice went still as Cendra wrapped her arms around her, holding her tight.

"I *will* find my answers, and I will come back to you. I swear it."

"Oh Cendra ..." Helene's heart broke and soared in equal measure as she embraced her daughter, weeping openly. "I am so, so very *proud* of you."

The flowers swayed in the breeze as the citizens gathered for Evocation, a memorial for the departed. The cobbles had been pried from the street where the blooms pushed up through the earth—the people of Esterby were building a makeshift shrine where they grew to honor Raure's sacrifice; not three days prior, he lay in this very spot. The dazzling blossoms had spread in a wide circle, radiating from where his body had landed. A mason had carved a little stone altar before the vibrant blooms; the engraving it bore read "Raure Irelos Memorial Garden." People placed ribbons and candles, notes of gratitude and plaques bearing the names of the friends and family lost in the battle.

Brandt wiped away a lone tear. "He would have hated this."

"No, you would have hated this," Fionna corrected. "He would have thought the fuss over him was silly ... but he'd have been laughing."

He chuckled softly. "Yes. ... I suppose you're right."

Brandt watched with concern as Tannah approached the altar. She had been particularly devastated by the loss, not uttering a single word since his passing. She stepped gently past the altar, taking care not to disturb the blooms. Reaching the center, she dug through Raure's satchel and produced a single seed. She pushed her finger into the earth, leaving a small hole into which she deposited the seed, then gently brushed dirt over it. Wordlessly, she returned to Brandt, staying close in his shadow. Together, the three waited as Cendra and Helene placed their candles before joining them.

In the back of the cart, nestled between a chest and their bags, Aska yawned lazily.

"I suppose it's time." Cendra's voice was solemn.

"Cart and horses are packed." Brandt took Helene's hand and gave it a firm shake. "Thank you for those, by the way."

"It is the least we could do. We will always be in your debt. I have no right to ask more, but I must. ... Please, take care of her."

Cendra embraced her mother one last time. "I can see to myself, mother. We'll be fine; we have each other."

Her mother smiled warmly. "Yes, you absolutely can. Be safe."

The group exchanged hugs and goodbyes, and Helene, Fionna, and the whole of Esterby waved goodbye as they passed through the gate.

As they crested the hill to the south of town, Cendra turned and watched as the townspeople drew the outer gate shut. Thoughts of the past came to her: a lifetime of memories—playing games in the streets as a child, long talks with her mom, friends now gone. Looking down on Esterby now, it looked so very different. It was smaller, somehow, and distant. She could have stayed; she could have stayed quite comfortably, in fact. The inheritance, long withheld from her, had been released, enough to provide herself an easy life. It would have been a hollow existence, however. What she had said was true; Esterby was no longer home. She recognized the faces, but they felt as if they had been worn by strangers. How ironic, she thought, after so much time longing for home that, now it welcomed her again with open arms, it was no longer where she needed to be. Far too many questions burned in her heart, questions longing desperately for answers. She could not be sure she had made the right choice, but at long last, the choice was hers to make.

She turned to the road ahead, a smile across her face.

It had taken two days, but Fionna had managed to sort the staggering collection of books and papers by subject. The collections included studies on history; works predating the oldest volumes she had seen, thought lost to time. The various artifacts Breoghan had collected shared only one trait in that they bore magic within them, their functions ranging from whimsical, to novel, to dangerous. She glanced around at the various piles, huffing at the sheer enormity of the task before her. She struggled at the thought of where to begin. Selecting a tome from the top of the history pile, she began to clear space on the old desk.

Something caught her eye. Peeking out from beneath the box of polished stones, a parchment—one that had escaped her notice until this moment. She slipped it out from beneath the box and scanned its contents.

Her eyes drew wide as she looked it over. The parchment was littered with glyphs she could not interpret, perhaps a far-off or long-dead language, but it also bore a sketch. A sketch of three stones set into pendants, each of similar size and shape. One was immediately familiar—the Heart of Armine.

Shit.

EPILOGUE

The Portrait in the Ruin

The heavens glowed red over Esterby, high on the hill above the cliffs as Breoghan exited the caves near the shore. He watched the sky burn with a measure of consternation; of the beasts he still held under the power of his stone, none should have been capable of destruction on such a scale.

No matter; one of barghests had retrieved the prize he long sought. He ran a finger over the stone; the Heart of Armine, its soft ruby light emanating from within, was his. The charade of years could, at long last, end.

His assuredness shook at an all-too-familiar sound: the thunderous beat of colossal wings on the air. He turned his gaze to Esterby high above and watched as the titanic reptilian beast took wing, hauling its tremendous form aloft.

Atenryth.

His eyes narrowed to a scowl. Now, nearly two decades hence, the beast had returned. There was no doubt it now hunted him.

Breoghan had hoped to study the stones further before using them in this manner, but no time remained. He would have to trust in what he had gleaned from the texts he had found. From his pocket, he produced a second stone. A pentagonal-faceted teardrop, its cut identical to its sister, but its color a brilliant sapphire blue—the Mind of Ilona. He could feel the stones pulling toward each other as he brought them slowly together, a soft hum ringing in his ears as they began to glow. The stones snapped together with a crystalline ringing, forming a long, octagonal pendant. He closed his eyes, clutching the pendant tight. The space around him warped and wavered, reality itself caving to the amulet's power—the space around him collapsed, and in a flash of violet light, Breoghan was gone.

ABOUT THE GRIFFIN BROTHERS

Scott and Doug grew up in the countryside near Havensville, Kansas with their parents and six other brothers and sisters. In the hills and prairies of Northeast Kansas, far outside the city imagination, was the truest kind of magic, and both brothers were prone to grand dreams and ideas.

As a child, Scott Griffin would often imagine elaborate stories of danger, mystery, and heroism while playing with his toys and action figures. That hobby would eventually evolve into creating worlds and stories for characters born of his own imagination.

Doug Griffin spent a great deal of his time immersed in the grand stories found in fantasy books, films, and video games. A lifelong fan of epic fantasy, he spent years building worlds and characters for his tabletop gaming friends.

This book is the first step into a larger adventure—one the Griffin Brothers are excited to embark upon with their readers.

ACKNOWLEDGMENTS

For their help in making this book a reality, we would like to thank:

Nick Perry at Redlegger Studio for cover art.

Adam and Regina Stephenson at Entsbough Publishing Services for copy editing and publishing support. There are 339 em dashes in this text. We did not type a single one correctly.

Xavier Strong for help in worldbuilding.

Elizabeth VanHoutan at Smothered in Ketchup and Andrew Howard at Round Table Bookstore for continual support and guidance.

And the following people who signed up to be beta readers: Judy Griffin, Steve Griffin, Renee Griffin, Dave Hemler, Bethany Clark, Jesse Ells, Holly Bowles, Annie Degenhardt, and Katy Watson.